YOU CANNOLI DIE ONCE

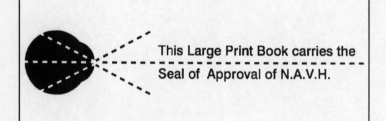

This Large Print Book carries the
Seal of Approval of N.A.V.H.

You Cannoli Die Once

Shelley Costa

THORNDIKE PRESS
A part of Gale, Cengage Learning

GALE
CENGAGE Learning·

Detroit • New York • San Francisco • New Haven, Conn • Waterville, Maine • London

Copyright © 2013 by Shelley Costa.
Thorndike Press, a part of Gale, Cengage Learning.

LIBRARY OF CONGRESS CATALOGING-IN-PUBLICATION DATA

Costa, Shelley.
    You Cannoli Die Once / By Shelley Costa. — Large Print edition.
        pages cm. — (Thorndike Press Large Print Mystery.)
    ISBN 978-1-4104-6222-0 (hardcover) — ISBN 1-4104-6222-6 (hardcover) 1.
Cooking, Italian—Fiction. 2. Restaurants—Fiction. 3. Grandparent and
child—Fiction. 4. Murder—Investigation—Fiction. 5. Pennsylvania—Fiction. 6.
Large type books. I. Title.
PS3603.O8664Y68 2013
813'.6—dc23   2013020397

Published in 2013 by arrangement with Pocket Books, a division of Simon & Schuster, Inc.

Printed in the United States of America
1 2 3 4 5 6 7 17 16 15 14 13

*In memory of my parents and
our beautiful years together*

ACKNOWLEDGMENTS

To Michael for more than I can say; Jess, Rebecca, and Liza for sharing in the fun; Marnie for plotting over scrambled eggs; Casey for being endlessly savvy about this business; Jerry for the legal stuff; my editor, Micki, for her good eyes and ears; my agent, John, for enthusiastically setting it all in motion; and all the friends, family, and readers who know what it means to me.

WELCOME TO MIRACOLO . . .

Eve Angelotta: The single, thirtysomething head chef runs Miracolo's kitchen with a cool head and a passionate heart. But creating northern Italian cuisine that makes people swoon is just one of her talents. Suddenly a sleuth after discovering a corpse on the kitchen tiles, Eve turns up the heat to prove her grandmother's innocence and serve a killer their just desserts.

Maria Pia Angelotta: She's not the kind of grandmother who makes brownies and sells crap on eBay. Larger than life, a beauty in her mid-seventies, the formidable owner of Miracolo has a soft side — hearing "Three Coins in the Fountain" makes Eve's nonna weep without fail. But where was Maria Pia when her boyfriend was murdered in cold blood?

Joe Beck: Digging through Miracolo's compost heap at midnight searching for his wedding ring doesn't exactly signal to Eve that this sexy, handsome lawyer is actually single — *or* sane. But after murder at Miracolo puts everything she loves on the line, Eve turns to Joe for advice, friendship, and more. . . . Is there anything else he's hiding from her?

Arlen Mather: The murder victim was Maria Pia's intimate, but how well did she know him? How did he get into Miracolo after hours? Who wielded the fatal blow to his head? And why was he found clutching a priceless opera artifact — a rare 78 rpm recording of Enrico Caruso singing in English — that had belonged to Eve's great-grandfather?

1

Monday

It was 11:53 p.m., and the late-night regulars showed no sign of leaving.

As I lovingly dried my utility knife, I shouldered open the kitchen's double doors and peeked into the dining room of Miracolo, our family-owned Italian restaurant. My great-grandfather had opened it back in 1937, and to hear the stories, you'd think he arrived by covered wagon instead of in a 1931 DeSoto.

Apparently Great-Granddad Alberto Camarata just had to get out of the wilds of Brooklyn and travel across the hostile territory of New Jersey before settling in Quaker Hills, Pennsylvania, forty minutes north of Philly. He felt such deliverance from whatever was driving him to leave New York that he named the place Miracolo, "miracle."

And the miracle business has been driving successive generations of cooking Camaratas and Angelottas crazy ever since. I now watched my grandmother, Maria Pia Angelotta, single-handedly provide the atmosphere here at Miracolo. To get the picture of Maria Pia, think Anne Bancroft with more wrinkles and bigger boobs. At nearly midnight, after a ten-hour work day, my seventy-six-year-old nonna — Italian for *grandmother* — was dancing.

This consisted of swaying her hips and waving her arms experimentally, because she'd once watched a movie about Isadora Duncan. *"Che bella ragazza"* — what a beautiful girl — she opined, "even if she wasn't Italian." Nonna didn't wear the perpetual old-world widow's weeds that pretty much resemble a Hefty bag with a white lace collar. Her black-clad hips were much more fashion forward, making it all the way to 1955 and those belted, full skirts sported by Lucy Ricardo.

I watched contentedly in the afterglow of my saltimbocca alla Eva — that's me, Eve Angelotta, head chef here at Miracolo — the veal special that had sold out early. It always does, which I attribute to the fact that I substitute tarragon for sage. Tarragon is user-friendly. Sage is . . . well, like a dancing grandmother who believes your purpose in life should be to find a nice Italian boy, get married, and produce future chefs for Miracolo.

While I inhaled the lingering aroma of the caper-tarragon gravy, Leo, one of the regulars, launched into a mandolin version of "Three Coins in the Fountain." This was bad news, because that song always undid Maria Pia to the extent that she'd start flinging herself around the dining room in full circles, which was alarming if you happened to be glassware.

"Is she weeping yet?" My cousin (and sous chef) Landon Angelotta slipped behind me, craning to peer into the dining room.

"Almost." Nonna always sobs at the line "Each heart longing for its home." Two lines later the songwriter rhymes *home* with *Rome* — that place in the south — so we suspect she must have had her heart broken by a Roman.

Landon reported: "And . . . there she goes."

I sighed.

But then our aged bartender, Giancarlo Crespi, dressed in his traditional red jacket, stepped out from behind the gleaming teakwood bar and stiffly approached my grandmother with a white linen napkin in his left hand. Some of the late-nighters whistled and pounded the tables that they always rearrange for the entertainment, and they all chimed in, singing the lyrics, a game I refer to as Find the Key. Was Giancarlo surrendering? Was he a matador with a death wish, approaching the bullish Maria Pia?

But no. Like the proud Genovese immigrant he was, he caught Maria Pia in a one-armed clasp, saving our glassware, and they improvised some wannabe sexy spin, circling his white linen napkin overhead. A real crowd-pleaser.

My friend Dana Cahill, who usually sings with the grappa-drinking music makers, was absent that night. When she's there, roaming around with her cordless mic, she and Maria Pia end up as dueling divas, their smiles frozen in place, but really trying to top each other with boisterous renditions of "Those Were the Days." Most evenings there are a couple of acoustic guitars, a mandolin, a homemade string bass, a tambourine, and bongos. Occasionally the clarinet shows up.

I gave skinny, dear Landon a quick hug and sent him out through the double doors. *"Buona notte, bellissimo,"* I whispered. He melted as nicely as the butter in his saucepan.

Dancing quickly across my beautiful black-and-white-tiled floor, I dreamed about my upcoming trip to the American Culinary Federation's annual convention in Orlando in three weeks. Nonna had seemed positively airy and magnanimous when she told me she'd pay for me to go.

As I placed my precious utility knife back in the block, I happened to glance out the long window behind the cavernous stainless steel sinks — and couldn't believe my eyes.

In the light of the half-moon, a man in floral swim trunks was standing on top of our compost bin. The five-foot-high wood enclosure is at the very back of the property, behind some flowering bushes at the end of the expansive dining courtyard that we open for dining every June first.

It looked like the guy had pulled over a wrought-iron patio chair to help himself up. And, from what I could tell, he was barefoot and edging his way around the front of the bin with something in his hands.

I silently opened the back door. The thumping bass from the open dining room windows, and the group bellowing a big finish to the Fountain song — "Make it mine! Make it mine! Make it mine!" — was why the compost man didn't hear me creep up on him, armed with the first thing I could grab near the kitchen door.

"What the hell are you doing?" I barked

15

in the voice I usually reserve for housebreaking pets.

He whirled, lost his footing, and went over with a whoop. Whatever he'd been holding in his hands clattered to the patio.

I pulled a tiki light over and saw him clinging to the inside rim of the compost bin. "I see you," I actually said.

"Well, I know you see me."

"Get out of there this instant."

His bare back was resting on what looked like rotting lettuce and potato peels from a couple of days ago. "Can you give me a hand?" he sputtered.

"You got yourself into this mess," I told him, stepping back and crossing my arms.

The next thing I knew, he was trying to haul himself up with a majestic grunt. In the moonlight there was something sinister in the way he slapped first a forearm and then a leg — a nicely shaped one, I might add — over the top of the bin. I held my breath as the rest of him came into sight like some creature emerging from the kind of sludge in those movies where everyone's hysterical in dubbed English.

"I've got a weapon!" I warned.

He squinted at me. "You've got a parasol."

I looked at my right hand. So I did — the pretty paper and bamboo one my dad had given me after a business trip to Japan, when I was fourteen. I scrambled over to his own weapon that had fallen onto the patio, and picked up . . . a metal detector. He was going through my compost in floral swim trunks with a metal detector? What kind of roving weirdo does that? I held on to the metal detector just in case.

As he rested on the rim, he asked, "Could I have the chair, please?"

Hmm — was that safe? Well, whatever was going to happen was going to happen. In the time it took me to run inside for the phone, he could be all over me. Besides, there was something about his comfort with the word *parasol* that worked in his favor.

I tugged the patio chair over with my leg, hopping on my other foot. I thought he said thank you, but only the compost could say for sure.

No movement.

"Are you hurt?" I didn't want a headline like that one a few years ago, where a burglar sued the homeowner because he got hurt during the commission of the crime.

"Just humiliated."

"Well." I widened my eyes at him. "And who brought that on?"

"And frustrated." He let out a huge sigh.

"Look," I said, shoving the chair right

underneath him, "I don't know what kind of fetish you have going on, but I want you to stay out of my garbage. Are we clear on that? You're trespassing —"

He showed a certain amount of grace — and an attractive bare chest — as he lowered himself to the chair. "Am I really, Eve?" He gave a quick push through his short hair, then looked me straight in the eye.

Violins blared like sirens. Hitchcock films crowded around. "How do you know my name?"

"You're Eve Angelotta, Miracolo's head chef."

Did he catch me on that *Good Neighbors* show on WYBE TV 35? Was I famous?

Then he went on kind of sheepishly, "To tell you the truth, I was here last night."

"What are you talking about?"

"With, well, you know, your cousin . . ."

Ah, my cousin, the organic farmer Kayla. I should have known.

Unless he meant Landon. I eyed him.

Brushing coffee grounds out of his hair, he told me his name was Joe Beck, lawyer brother of the hunky florist James Beck three doors up from Miracolo. (He didn't actually say "hunky.") He had just moved out from Philly a couple of months ago and was helping in the shop this week whenever he could fit it in between clients. He had met my cousin Kayla during one of her early-morning power walks. I didn't want to tell him that Kayla had probably seen him around, fancied him, and spun him a tale about regular exercise that I knew never happened.

"One thing led to another —" he said.

"And you ended up here."

On the leather couch in the office, was my guess.

He squinted at me in the glare of the tiki light, but since I stood in the shadows, he wouldn't be able to see my face clearly. His own was pretty good, if you overlooked the bit of zucchini on his forehead. Everything about him was wry — the mouth, the eyes, even the nose, which veered off a little at the end. The hair just did a trim dark blond thing with a golden assist from the moonlight.

I waited.

"Well, it's kind of embarrassing."

"For you, maybe."

"Kayla didn't think you'd mind," he said.

"No, Kayla didn't think I'd know." She just might lose key privileges over this. "How many nights?"

He seemed to study the trumpet vine on the stockade fence. "Three." Then he said,

"It seemed to run its course," which was an uncannily accurate way of describing my cousin's viral love life.

I finally handed him his metal detector. "What were you looking for?"

He slung the metal detector over his shoulder, then gave me a two-fingered salute. "My wedding ring," he said, and disappeared through the gate.

I twirled my pink paper parasol and headed back to the kitchen.

From inside the dining room came the opening finger picks of "My Heart Will Go On," played on two guitars. It sounded like someone had actually brought a pan flute — although I had often witnessed the mandolin-playing Leo cup his hands to his mouth and make a sound like a loon. Pretty, either way.

Tuesday

On the morning of May 27, my life seemed to be scored by an Oscar-winning composer:

A good-looking compost invader at midnight.

A job I loved, although I'd never admit it to Nonna.

A new satin-and-lace camisole in chocolate brown from my favorite boutique down the street, Airplane Hangers.

A new shampoo that delivered shine, volume, and coverage — everything I like in a man but with fewer complications.

So it felt particularly unfair when I let myself into Miracolo at 1:21 p.m., singing Lionel Ritchie's "Endless Love" in a lavish falsetto, and strode into my kitchen. Whereupon something looked terribly out of place.

Maybe it was the body on the floor.

What looked like an older man, sprawled on his stomach, wearing khaki pants and a yellow short-sleeved summer shirt. When I tried to see past all the blood, I noticed that his head was bashed in. Skulls that look like that are pretty much done working the *Times* crossword puzzle, not to mention finding any kind of a hat that fits.

I started shaking.

I staggered over to the wall, where I meant to turn on the lights, but flipped the switch that started the loop of Sinatra music. "My Way" started, and my eyes slid back to the dead guy.

Regrets, I've had a few, but then again, too few to mention . . .

Melting against the wall, I killed the music and looked around the empty Miracolo kitchen, trembling.

Who did this? And why here, in my place?

My nonna might own the restaurant,

swanning around chatting up the regulars and sampling my sauces while trying to convince me I'll never "catch a man" wearing pants (to which I counter, "How about one wearing a skirt?"), but Miracolo felt like mine.

I pushed myself off the wall and looked more closely at the dead guy, afraid it was somebody I knew — some delivery guy, a regular customer, ex-boyfriend, or maybe even my so-called father. He'd been gone for so many years I wasn't sure I'd recognize him. We were pretty sure his farewell note, "I can't take her anymore," referred to his mother, Maria Pia.

The guy had short, thick white hair and his face had a kind of hard, rubbery look. His eyes were glazed, like he was trying to look out from behind frosted glass. And his mouth was frozen in a look that seemed to say, *I'm not sure this is quite what I had in mind for today.*

One thing was for sure: I didn't know him. Had never seen him before.

This was an immense relief.

So why were my hands still shaking?

Just tell yourself it's like having a misdelivered package. Call someone who can come take him away, preferably in the next five minutes, before Landon —

"Someone's in the kitchen with E-e-eve," sang out Landon.

Too late.

"Someone's in the kitchen, I know-oh-oh-oh." Then he flipped on all the overhead lights . . . and shrieked.

2

"Landon, Landon, calm down," I pleaded.

"Don't tell me to calm down!" His eyes looked wild.

"Stop shrieking," I said, grabbing his arms.

"I'm not shrieking!"

"Yes, you are."

Landon was wearing a turquoise unitard under the black pants that are part of the Miracolo "look." He has a Tuesday-morning theater dance class in Philly, where he signs in as Landon Michaels, his hopeful stage name. But at this moment he didn't look like he could remember any of his names.

I pointed to the dead body. "Can we focus, please?"

He cautiously ventured a few steps toward me. "Who's the poor unfortunate?"

"I don't have any idea. He was here when I arrived — but I keep thinking he's meant to be somewhere else."

24

Landon looked at me anxiously. "Like someone got it wrong?"

"Exactly!"

"Because why would someone dump their — business — in Miracolo? I mean, it's not like we're a construction site or anything."

"Or the Pine Barrens."

We both shuddered.

"Do you think this is related to the string of local break-ins?" he hissed.

In the last three months, a rug shop on the far side of Market Square and an antique shop on East Tenth Street had been robbed. "I don't know. I don't think so. Doesn't this seem kind of . . . worse?"

He suddenly sucked in about a quart of air, and then jiggled his fingers mutely.

"What?" I whirled.

"There's the — the — weapon."

"Where?"

And then I saw it. About a foot away from the body was the black marble mortar I use for grinding spices. I heroically thrust out an arm to hold Landon back, as if the mortar were capable of independent movement.

"Well. That changes things. It means he wasn't dumped here." Oh, God.

"He wasn't?" Landon's green eyes were the size of the spangles on my old purple velvet belly dancing belt, back in my former professional life as a dancer.

"No. He was killed here," I announced, violating my rule about not speaking with authority about anything I'm clueless about — which pretty much sets me apart from half of the Angelottas and all of the Camaratas.

I sent Landon out front to call 911 and our cousin Choo Choo Bacigalupo — I found myself needing Choo Choo's bald, 300-pound presence to reassure me that the world was still filled with things like fine Italian pastries, and told him to leave informing our nonna to me. If I delegated that to him, the two of them together could give hysteria a bad name.

I stepped away from our "poor unfortunate," wondering how he — and his killer — had gotten into our restaurant. While I waited for the cops, I mindlessly scooped up some fallen silver sugar pearls that Landon used when he made a cassata cake yesterday, and brushed them off onto the junk mail we throw into the corner of the junk counter.

And when I turned back, that's when I noticed that the dead guy was lying on one of our Caruso records.

■ ■ ■ ■

Before saving enough money to open Miracolo in 1937, Great-Granddad chauffeured
around a Metropolitan Opera tenor. When
the tenor had to blow town — publicly tout-
ing the glories of Il Duce, Mussolini, led to
the haste — he presented his chauffeur with
his personal collection of 78s. One of the
rarities was a recording of "Your Eyes Have
Told Me What I Did Not Know," the only
song recorded in English by Enrico Caruso.

I had mounted a few shadow boxes holding opera memorabilia on the beautiful old
brick walls lining Miracolo's dining room,
and Caruso singing in English was my prize.

It was all I could do not to slide the
precious record out from under the dead
guy's hips before it ended up as evidence,
crammed into some dark file cabinet at the
police station. Cracked into five helpless
pieces. That record hadn't survived flooded
basements, lousy housekeeping, even a
small house fire, over the course of four
generations, only to get tossed willy-nilly
into an evidence box.

At the sound of raised voices, I left the
kitchen.

The inner door to Miracolo opened to a

chorus of gasps, revealing Landon's back and what looked like my rubbernecking cousin Kayla and my pal Dana Cahill, carrying on like they were waiting for the doors to open for one of Loehmann's especially competitive sales. I pulled the inner door shut and walked over to them.

To hear Kayla babble, you'd think the unpleasantness described by Landon was somehow affecting the entire escarole crop on the East Coast.

But Dana just asked me softly, "Problem?"

Dana's one of those supremely confident people who never seems to need long hours of girlfriend therapy involving margaritas and prank calls to loser men. Her husband, Patrick, owns an entire block of buildings on Market Square, though not ours — which keeps things friendly and simple.

I folded my arms across my chef jacket and started to answer their questions, like would I say it's more gruesome than ghastly, how deep is the dent in the skull, and just how close I might be to puking up my breakfast.

And then, suddenly my face froze. Except for my lower lip, which started to quiver. Oh, no. Not here. Not now. *Not ever.* Five years ago, I had survived a fall that broke my leg in two places and pretty much ended my Broadway dancing career, without blubbering. And I'd survived Nonna's triumph when — broke and a little bit broken — I had capitulated and joined the family business.

Dana stepped up close, but then Dana always steps up close. Her sense of her own personal space lies well within your own. Most days, I don't mind. She pushed a lock of my wavy chestnut hair behind my ear. "Tough morning, darling? Shall I run to Starbucks and get you something with lots of foam?"

Really, the terrible thing about kindness is that it comes when you most need it.

My shoulders slumped . . . and I started bawling. Then I flung myself, wailing, at Dana and the Versace scarf around her neck. Landon and Kayla closed in, going for a group hug that yielded a veritable potpourri of Lady Speed Stick (Kayla), Skin So Soft (Landon), and Opium (guess who) applied a little freely for early afternoon.

As I heard dueling sirens wail to a stop outside Miracolo, I came to my senses. "Landon, grab the bag from the butcher. It's just inside the kitchen doors. *Quick!*" A bag holding ten pounds of flank steak for braciole sitting out on the murder floor, where I'd dropped it earlier, wouldn't survive who knew how many days of the Quaker Hills version of *CSI*.

Landon broke away from the group force field and disappeared in a dash of turquoise through the inner door. My cousin Kayla started spouting harebrained theories about the identity of the dead guy and motives for the crime, while Dana pulled a compact out of her handbag. The two of them took turns checking hair and lipstick, baring their teeth to expose any seeds or spinach still hanging around after lunch.

We couldn't afford to close down for days while the cops did their thing behind yellow crime scene tape, but what could we do? "Landon, hurry," I called, then peeked out the street door as two black-and-whites disgorged four cops to the sound of radio crackle.

I was just about to head them off at the pass — do a little meet-and-greet out there on the sidewalk — when Landon sprang back into our little group, brandishing the bag of flank steak. I fell back, mashing poor Dana's left foot, and took a huge breath when the street door swung open.

The marines had landed.

They dutifully checked out for themselves that there was indeed a dead guy in the restaurant, where, I reflected, the previous most exciting thing was the time I had sex in the back office with the FedEx guy. Although that had turned out to be one of those "what was I thinking?" moments, at least what happened in the back office stayed in the back office.

We spilled out onto Market Square.

It was a warm early afternoon in late May and a few lunch stragglers still loitered under the green awning at Sprouts, the vegetarian café two doors down.

Dana rubbed all of our shoulders.

Landon practiced some *pas de bourrée.*

I shredded a croissant and stuffed the flaky pieces in my mouth. Landon had to remind me to chew.

Kayla stood utterly still with her eyes closed. I could swear I heard her annoying mantra — *noof* — buzzing around us. Or maybe she was just winding up a good *malocchio* — the Italian evil eye — against the murderer responsible for shutting down Miracolo before she got paid.

Dana chewed her French-manicured nails and watched me pace.

A crowd, of course, gathered.

And a man sauntered to a stop. "Hello, Kayla."

It was Joe Beck, dressed today in jeans

31

and a well-worn orange and gray plaid shirt. Landon murmured something about a blond Ryan Reynolds, and Dana countered with something about Eric Bana, only subtract the waves and add a dimple a girl could disappear into like Alice down the rabbit hole. All of which I think Joe heard. Although I happened to agree with her about the dimple, I kept it to myself.

First, corpses.

Now the real embarrassment: my friends and family.

"Joseph," Kayla said with a flip of her newly colored red and professionally curled hair.

That seemed to conclude the joyful re-union between the two lovers. Somehow I expected more from people who, for three nights, had shared the ultimate intimacy — underwear — together. But about this Beck guy, I knew next to nothing except he scares easily and can tell the difference between a parasol and an umbrella.

He was taking in the cop cars, the crowd, and me. "Carbon monoxide?" He turned his blue eyes to me inquiringly.

"Dead guy," I said and crossed my arms. "Smashed skull. We have good monoxide detectors."

"Yeah," he said thoughtfully. "Those won't

help much with blunt objects."

"Mortar and pestle," I added. "Well, just the mortar."

Joe Beck crossed his arms. "So who is he?"

"Don't know him, never saw him."

Joe Beck thrust out his lower lip kind of skeptically, I thought. Then he gave a little shrug. "Why would some total stranger —"

Just then a girl in pink spandex, with enough metal on her face to jam navigation systems everywhere, sidled up from the crowd and gave him a gum-chewing once-over, followed by a thumbs-up, which made him smile.

Kayla started unloading vegetables from the back of her blue van emblazoned in yellow script with Kale & Kayla Organics, the name of her farm. "Wait, wait, Kayla!" What was I going to do with five crates of egg-plants, escarole, peppers —

Dana started answering the crowd's morbid questions about the dead guy, though of course she had no answers.

Choo Choo. Where was Choo Choo? He was good at crowd control.

Kayla hauled another crate out of the back of the van of plenty. "Kayla, stop," I yelled, "I can't possibly —"

Joe Beck shifted his weight and tried again. "Why would some total stranger break into Miracolo just to shuffle off this mortal coil?"

I put my hands on the hips that were somewhere under the chef jacket. Doesn't anybody design alluring chef wear? "Are you saying the guy's a suicide?" I shot him a challenging look. "Then how come his head was bashed in when I found him lying on 'Your Eyes Have Told Me What I Did Not Know'?"

Joe looked confused. "What's 'Your Eyes Have Told Me —' "

I stood up straighter. " 'Your Eyes Have Told Me,' " I said in my prissiest manner, "is a song recorded by Enrico Caruso in 1925. In English. The only one. It's a treasure in opera memorabilia."

"I'll take your word for it."

I checked out the rest of us refugees from the family business. What on earth was I going to do with them? Being barred from the restaurant for a couple of days was going to be a serious problem. What about payroll? I groaned.

"Well," said Joe, "your day is pretty effectively screwed."

I gaped. "And people pay you for that kind of insight?"

"Four hundred an hour."

"I guess it's easy to mistake cost for

value." Oops, out of my mouth before I could stop it.

He started to laugh.

Which made me stamp my foot. "I've got to interview an applicant for the pianist position in forty-five minutes, and no place to do it now — let alone a piano!"

"You can use James's other room while the cops sample the physical evidence in your restaurant. He's away at the Chelsea Flower Show in the UK. How's that?"

"Well," I sighed, "I'll have to see the space first."

"Of course." He jerked his dark blond head toward the flower shop. "Come on."

I turned to check on Dana and my cousin Kayla. The crowd had increased; I saw Adrian the bouncer from Jolly's Pub across the square, a frazzled old man in a gray overcoat and apparently nothing else, and a few wandering Goths who hadn't heard just how far out of Philly or style they had gone.

"Kayla, I can't use any of this," I shouted at her. "Take it all back —"

An unmarked car pulled up and double-parked alongside one of the black-and-whites. Out climbed what I'd put money on being two detectives, one a tall blond woman in boots, the other a man in jeans and a linen sport coat. They spotted Joe

Beck right away.

"Joe," the male said, looking at our stranded little group.

"Ted," said Joe.

We could all take lessons from male conversations.

"Sally," added Joe.

She adjusted her sweater, which took all of her attention. Plus Adrian's. Then: "Joe."

The Ted guy took out a battered spiral notebook and addressed our group. "Which one of you" — his eyes slowed at Landon — "is Evelyn Angelino?"

The name confusion thing wouldn't bother me so much if I hadn't gone out of my way to become a household word. If you happened to be in the audience during the October 23, 2009, performance of *Mary Poppins* at the New Amsterdam Theatre, you'll remember the header that poor unfortunate dancer Eve Angelotta took off the stage during "Step in Time."

Backstory? The sudden and colossal onset of an oncoming head cold, followed by being handed an antihistamine backstage by a fellow dancer. Considering I never take anything, not even vitamins, when "Step in Time" started, my legs felt like logs disconnected from my body. All I could do was watch those logs with a kind of horrified but dozy detachment while I tried to pump my prop chimney brush, which now felt like trying to bench-press a utility pole.

Long story short, I stepped clear off the stage (cue horrified screams from the seats), asleep with my eyes open. The fast-thinking dance captain, Tony Treadwell, followed me with a back flip and pulled me out of a broken-legged sprawl. With Tony propping me up, we struck a toothy pose to everyone's amazement and delight. The paramedics managed to collect me through the orchestra pit and nobody was the wiser.

So whenever somebody calls me Evie Angeletti or Ava Angelo or Evelyn Angelino, I bristle. What does a girl have to do to become a household word?

Sighing, I sent Landon, Dana, and Kayla across the square to Jolly's Pub, where I hoped the classy older man who owned it, Reginald Jolly, would at least give them a drink on the house. Then I told Ted, nope, I don't know who the dead guy is. Nope, I don't know how the dead guy got inside; the door was locked when I got there. Nope, I have no idea why he's lying on our Caruso record. A crazed collector?

After a bunch of other questions the detective released me temporarily, so I went up the street to Flowers by Beck, lugging ten pounds of flank steak. Joe showed me the back room where James apparently taught ikebana classes, and I decided that it would do.

When the bell over the front door tinkled, I followed Joe into the front room. While he waited on a customer in a gray business suit, I prowled the shop and came to a stop in front of the refrigerator.

Perfect! Thirty seconds later, my ten pounds of flank steak were the new neighbor to a pail of lavender roses, red and pink Oriental lilies, and spotted gold orchids. Ted had told me we'd have to close for a day, maybe two, while techs went over the crime scene, and I wasn't about to let this prime meat go to waste.

When this was all over, I'd thank Joe with a dinner at Miracolo. The risotto. It's the cheapest thing on the menu.

While the customer was looking around to decide what he wanted, Joe produced an electric keyboard from his brother's storage space upstairs, where they stashed instruments the two of them had bought and tried, so if I also had a sudden need for steel drums or a xylophone, I knew where to come.

I was threading my way through the floor

displays to return to Miracolo, to post a note to the pianist applicant on our front door, when the flower shop's bell tinkled again.

In walked Detective Sally, with a troubled look on her face. "Ms. Angelotta?" Close on her heels were Dana, Landon — looking as taut as rubber bands on a rotisserie chicken — and our monumental maître d', my cousin Choo Choo Bacigalupo.

Out of the corner of my eye I saw Joe pause in giving the customer his change.

"Yes?" I said.

She held up a black leather billfold. "We've got the victim's ID. His name is Arlen Mather. Does that ring any bells?"

I staggered backward from the bad news, knocked over a four-tiered display of African violets and, in a crash of broken pottery, went down, down, down.

Arlen Mather was my grandmother's boy-friend.

3

Sally squinted down at me on the floor. "Your grandmother's boyfriend, and you don't know him?" she said in a testy kind of way.

I said the only thing that would explain it. "She's from Genoa." Choo Choo and Joe grabbed me by my arms and pulled me to my feet. Since Sally didn't seem to get the point, I went on, "They don't talk." Then I added: "They cook and they paint and they go to sea."

Dana looked at me quizzically. "I thought Maria Pia was born outside Philly?"

Merriam Webster, un·help·ful, *adj.: see* Dana. "She was, but her *family*'s from Genoa. It's the same thing."

Sally fixed me with a skeptical look. "That still doesn't explain why you don't know —"

I sighed. "Maria Pia is very private about . . . the things she's very private about." Hearing myself, I winced. If only this detective knew my grandmother, she wouldn't even bother with the question. I ask you, what good's a reputation if it doesn't give you a pass in the crazy department? Has this Sally person never been to Miracolo? Doesn't she eat?

I exchanged a look with Landon, who was crouched in the carnage of African violets, picking up shards of pottery.

"I completely get it," put in Dana, bumping up against me in her beige silk pants.

As I gave Detective Sally my grandmother's name and contact information, I thought about poor, konked Arlen Mather, who would never again be able to sample Maria Pia's, er, delights.

Joe clapped a hand on my quivering shoulder and told me I could clean myself up in the workroom in the back. Then he started to sweep the mess into a pile. I pulled the broom from his hand, telling him, "My mess, my sweep." Then I sniffed and added, "And my bill."

"No problem."

The blond detective jiggled her pencil, which looked as nibbled as her nails. And mine. "Who has a key to your restaurant?"

Holding their collective breath, Dana, Landon, and Choo Choo turned to me, as

41

wide-eyed as a colony of meerkats. They must have felt the awful truth coming before I even thought it through. "I have two. The one on my key ring, and the spare I keep at Jolly's for emergencies."

The meerkats were nodding their approval.

"Then Mar-Jo Properties has one — that's our landlord." I held up three fingers. Then my mind slowed down, with no more obvious key holders to report. No pianist yet, no needy, possessive boyfriends, no —

Wait.

"Kayla!" I blurted.

But then Landon held up a finger. "No, no," he announced, "just yesterday I saw Kayla hand over a key to —"

And we all watched while his poor face lost all expression.

"Yes?" intoned Sally.

"To our nonna." We could hardly hear him. "Kayla was returning Maria Pia's key."

"But that's for the Quaker Hills Cookbook Club," I warbled. "A book club for food geeks. They meet the first Tuesday morning of the month, and they critique the recipes in all the newest cookbooks." Was I in full babble mode yet? "Then they all eat egg-white omelets with asiago cheese that Nonna prepares. She's the club treasurer."

Was nobody moving?

Or, for that matter, breathing?

Sally snapped her notebook shut, turned on her stylish boot heels, and left, throwing something back to me about more questioning later.

Landon handed Joe Beck the broken pieces he had picked up.

Dana stroked my hair behind my ear again.

Choo Choo, in a hoodie as big and green as all the Poconos, whispered, "It doesn't mean she did it, you know." Which is the first time that thought got voiced. That Nonna might have done it.

"We'll clear her name," announced Dana in the evangelical voice she had used three years ago as the lead in *Anything Goes* at the local Windmill Theater. "And we'll do it starting now." Because Maria Pia has one of those combustible personalities that wouldn't come across well once the cops started to dig.

My cousins got noisily on board, but Choo Choo, scowling through his carefully trimmed scruff, looked grim and fatalistic. I thought it would probably take more than us to clear our beloved nonna's name, but we were the place to start. Landon announced a potluck at his condo that evening

43

at seven, with only happy food allowed — whatever that was.

Then I told them all, "Now go help Kayla take all her produce to the farmer's market. And don't forget to invite her to the pot-luck." That call to arms mobilized the three of them, and they left the Beck flower shop.

Once they were out of sight, my shoulders dropped and I turned to Joe. "I can't afford four hundred dollars an hour," I said quietly.

Joe Beck pursed his lips. "You may not need to. Let's see where the investigation goes." He plucked a mashed pink violet from my sleeve. "If you do end up needing legal help, I offer a good-neighbor dis-count."

My throat started to close up. "Since when?"

"That's not the right question."

My voice slid up toward the crybaby range. "Then what's the right question?"

" 'Joe, will you show me where I can get cleaned up?' "

"That's good," I managed, shielding my eyes with my hand, but not before he noticed my tears and got all awkward.

He patiently stared at the embossed tin ceiling while I held up a finger, then my whole hand, followed by two fingers pressed to my lips, then my whole fist like you do

44

when you try not to burp. He read the hand signals just right. "Take your time," he said, shoving his hands in his pockets.

I wasn't sure time was going to make any difference. Because whether it was now or days from now, all I could think of was that my grandmother had a key to Miracolo — and a murdered boyfriend inside.

These were the choices: Drive across town to hold my grandmother's hand and tell her about Arlen Mather before the cops came calling. Or . . . go through with the interview and audition of the only applicant for the pianist job at our cop-overrun restaurant.

I made the only possible decision.

After leaving the pianist, Mrs. Bryce Crawford, a voice mail about the change of venue, I downed one of the falafels Joe Beck bought from Sprouts after he set up the keyboard in the ikebana classroom, then turned the door sign to Closed and left to meet a client.

I figured we needed a pianist more than Nonna needed me to hold her hand. She was a curiously unsentimental woman. So I let myself off the tell-Nonna-her-beau's-got-a-little-less-on-his-mind-lately hook for the time being. And though it's a terrible thing to say, I didn't put it past her to be secretly thrilled to have such a dramatic story to tell over customers' tiramisus.

She'd be okay.

She'd . . . be okay.

Then I growled the growl I usually save for Nonna when she's being her most maddening, pulled out my phone, and left her the weirdest voice mail ever. "Just a heads-up, Nonna. Your boyfriend has turned up beaned" — wait, don't hold out false hope that she could be schlepping stuffed artichokes to an ICU somewhere — "and *killed* in the restaurant. I'm really sorry to tell you all this in a voice mail, Nonna, but I wanted to let you know to expect the cops on your doorstep anytime now." How on earth do you end a message like that? "Sorry," I muttered lamely, then hung up.

I was determined that Mrs. Crawford, whoever she turned out to be, would not pad away from here in her tan orthopedic shoes and Church Lady coif without having signed my employment contract. Even if her piano skills went no further than "Bringing in the Sheaves" and "The Phantom of the Opera," she was mine. At this point I could live with anything.

And then, she arrived.

"Is this the place for the piano audition?" said a deep, nasal voice.

I stopped playing my two-handed "Chopsticks" and eyed her. She was a tall woman dressed in a lime-green cocktail dress and matching heels. Plunging neckline, wide-brimmed hat, white fishnet gloves, black-and-lime square shoulder bag.

"Temporarily." I stood and thrust my hand at her. "A spot of trouble up the street at the restaurant." Although "spot of trouble" sounded less like homicide and more like a deep-fryer malfunction. "I'm Eve Angelotta, the head chef."

"Mrs. Bryce Crawford." Now that we were in handshake range, I saw she had the shoulders of a linebacker, wiry hair of strangely indeterminate color, and what could only be pancake makeup over her face and neck. Nicely blended. Red lip liner, coral lipstick. The fake eyelashes were like awnings over her pale green eyes.

"And may I call you . . . Bryce?"

She didn't even blink. "You may call me Mrs. Crawford."

"Of course." Maybe I should head over to give Nonna the bad news, after all . . .

She peeled off her gloves, slapping one lightly on the keyboard. "Is this the instrument I'll be using?"

"Only for the audition. There's a Yamaha U1 in the restaurant."

47

"Mm," Mrs. Bryce Crawford observed noncommittally.

I handed her a ballpoint pen and an application for employment, which she filled out on the counter by the cash register. Then we sat almost knee to knee in folding chairs used for the ikebana classes, while I tried to look employerlike as I glanced at her application.

She crossed her legs, which had been recently waxed. The heels were four inches, easy. Mrs. Crawford gave a Northeast Philly address, three clubs where she'd played most recently — not a church on the list — and a degree in piano performance from Berklee College of Music. No year. But then, I hadn't asked. What I was mostly aware of, as I looked between the lime-green Amazon looking at me inscrutably and the application form, was a very serious omission.

Gender.

Not a deal breaker.

Not when she played "Tiger Rag" like it was the last piece either of us would hear in this lifetime, so it had better be great. When she finished, I clapped like I used to when I was hysterical that Tinkerbell would die, pushed the contract at her, explained I couldn't pay her anywhere near what she was worth, and signed her up.

As she slipped on her white fishnet gloves and adjusted the wide-brimmed hat, I trotted to the refrigerator out front and pulled out a single lavender rose, which I presented to her. Mrs. Crawford lifted an eyebrow, inclined her head, and turned on her dyed-to-match heels.

I watched her head north on Market Square, past Akahana the Japanese bag lady, making her wandering way along the wide sidewalk, past Mr. von Veltheim the baker, adjusting his blue awning, past the Bucks County Community College student twosomes.

I cleaned up the rest of the wreckage of violets, cramming plants into new pots I found stashed in the back room, and swept. The four-tiered display stand was now a three-tiered display stand, but other than that, it didn't look too bad. Maybe my good-neighbor discount would apply to the violets . . .

While I swept, I wondered about the keys to Miracolo.

One was on my key chain. But what about the one I stashed at Jolly's? I suddenly felt queasy about it, but there was nothing I could do until I got through my to-do list.

49

As I swept the last of the spilled potting soil out the front door, I gazed longingly at Sprouts, where the tunes of Joni Mitchell escaped from the doorway.

If I sniffed really hard, I swear I could smell the lentil salad.

And then my cell phone rang. I pulled it out of the bar apron I had found on a hook in the back room and flipped it open.

" 'O blind lust! O foolish wrath! Who so dost goad us on —' " my grandmother began oratorically.

Oh, God, not Dante. He was her fallback guy, the go-to poet she turned to in life's toughest moments. (Me, I read bumper stickers.) She liked him so much she even forgave him for being born in Florence, which fell south of my Genovese grandmother's weird equivalent of a Mason-Dixon line.

"Nonna?" I took a breath. "I'm glad you called." So, two new things in one day. Dealing with dead bodies, happy to hear from difficult grandmother. I glanced down the street, where one of the black-and-white cop cars had left, replaced by the coroner's van.

But she wasn't done. I could picture her eyes closed as she went on poetizing about ramparts and centaurs, and although I couldn't quite find the connection — unless

Arlen had features I was unaware of — I could tell it was her way of memorializing her boyfriend. I just had to wait her out.

"Oh, Eve," she said as she abandoned the recital, "my poor Arlen."

Her voice sounded so small that my heart started pounding. Maria Pia is nothing if not larger than life. "I'm sorry, Nonna," I said, feeling helpless. This kind of comfort might be beyond me. "Since I never met Arlen, I didn't recognize him." *Dented like a can of cannellini on my kitchen floor.* "I mean, you weren't seeing him all that long, right?"

"In some ways I've known Arlen forever, Eve. He was a soul older than old. A soul that dragged itself out of the primordial . . ." Here her vocabulary failed her and she finished with, "whatnot."

Some of that primordial whatnot was on my kitchen floor.

"I get the idea, Nonna." Couldn't I have a grandmother who made brownies and sold crap on eBay?

All of a sudden her voice dropped and she sounded urgent. "Eve, *cara mia,* I have to see you. I have to talk to you."

"Sure. I've got some time after four." Must call the waitstaff, the uniform vendors, the carpet cleaners, the wholesalers —

"It's *important.*" She sounded like I was

51

arguing with her. "I don't know how much longer I can —"

"I promise I'll come by as soon as I can, but right now I've got to go, Nonna."

"I can't possibly see you today, Eve," she huffed. "What are you thinking? I need time to grieve."

I rolled my eyes. "I understand."

"Come tomorrow. Early. Say, eight. I've got a nine o'clock massage."

So she'd wedge grief in between espresso shots and hot stones.

"Darling, ever since I heard the news" — what, an hour ago? — "my back has felt as — as — clumped as that *strega* Belladonna Russo's *panna cotta.*" The witch in question, Belladonna Russo, was her cooking archrival in New Brunswick, New Jersey. Maria Pia expelled a breath that sounded like the first wind of all time. "And I'm not in the mood for lunch."

I pressed my lips together. "Murder's a terrible thing."

"So's prison," she said with a trace of the Philly accent and attitude she had worked hard to get past. And then she hung up.

4

Jolly's Pub is one of those pleasantly dark places you look for when you decide to go out for intrigue with somebody you'd rather not see too closely. Me, I go solo, for the Sam Adams Boston lager and the beer nuts. Not that I tell Maria Pia that. Hearing that anyone makes even a single non-Italian food choice produces such a look of hurt bafflement in her, you'd swear she'd just heard that Enrico Caruso was really a Hungarian mezzo-soprano named Magda who just had a very good costumer.

There was a long bar that gleamed like a grand piano and, even though it was only 4 p.m., the empty café tables were dotted with fake candles. In the warm weather, the entire glass front wall is moved up and out of sight, like a garage door, and the crowd spills out onto Market Square.

Reginald Jolly, a tall, lean Brit somewhere in his seventies, sat at a table in the darkest corner, working on what looked to be a schedule.

I led with, "You heard?"

"I heard." He set down his pen. "Big trouble at your place, eh?" Reginald had a pencil mustache even when pencil mustaches weren't cool, which was pretty much always. His stand on facewear filled me with confidence in the man, and if I couldn't honestly say I'd trust him with my life, I did at least trust him with my key.

"I'll say."

He made a move out of his seat. "A Laphroaig on the house?"

He has a fine line of single malts. Better than Miracolo's. "Does the queen like corgis?" I asked in our little routine. While he slipped behind the bar and reached for the bottle, I stared at one of his framed maps of this blessed plot, this earth, this realm, this England.

"So, Eve," he said, setting down the two shot glasses, then tugging at his creased pants legs as he sat, "what brings you across the street?" We picked up our drinks and touched our glasses together in the faintest of clinks.

Since he didn't seem to want any of the gruesome details about the discovery of poor Arlen, I blew right past it. "Just doing a little key inventory." I sipped the smoky Scotch.

He lifted his eyebrows at me.

"You still have the spare key?" It wasn't really a question.

Reginald did his one-shoulder shrug that never alters the line of his blindingly white shirt. "The key you gave me, yes?"

"Yeah. You have it, right?"

"I keep it locked in the smallest drawer in my office desk."

This is what I wanted to hear. Trust the guy with the pencil mustache anytime.

"Wonderful." I smiled and started to down the rest of my Laphroaig.

"Until that one bird came for it, oh, two weeks ago."

My heart sank. "What?"

"The one you sent to get the key. So they could practice in the mornings."

I couldn't believe what I was hearing. "Practice?" Practice what? *Who?*

"You didn't send her?" He dabbed his mouth with a cocktail napkin.

"No. No, I didn't. What did she look like?" What if it wasn't even someone I knew? How would I ever figure out who had my spare key?

Reginald narrowed his eyes, thinking back. "She was what you would call petite, with straight dark hair that comes to here" — a motion under his chin — "narrow shoulders, slim hips" — I could tell he was warming to his subject — "a woman no more than forty. She had a voice that was soft like good cashmere, but with a steel pipe wrapped up inside."

I sat staring blindly.

For the life of me, I couldn't figure out why Dana Cahill had tricked him into giving her my spare key.

Did she think I wouldn't find out?

Or was she hoping to return the key first?

I was baffled.

While I stood outside, leaning against the wall between Jolly's Pub and Tattie's, a souvenir shop, trying to figure out a next move that did not involve killing Dana, certain things happened on Market Square.

Across the street at Miracolo, all the official city cars were gone — and with them, Arlen Mather. While I'd been cleaning up my African violet mess, the coroner's van must have roared off in a wash of May sunlight.

Even Flasher Man had moved on, probably heading toward Pensey Park, a mile south, where he could do his best work. And Ted the detective had stopped by the flower shop to give me a receipt for "Your Eyes Have Told Me What I Did Not Know," which somehow didn't fill me with confidence.

Akahana was working her serpentine way back down the street, stopping to check out any trash can that might yield dinner. And young boys fell out of the front door of Head in the Game, a video-game emporium just down the street from Miracolo. At that moment, a slim brunette with an alligator-skin headband holding back her shoulder-length hair, wearing a green see-through shirt with a ruffled collar and black silk pants, and carrying a spangled handbag big enough to hold a small African nation, arrived at Flowers by Beck.

The way she worked the key in two seconds flat, opened the door, and disappeared inside led to some pretty fine detection. This was not a cleaning service. This was a wife. So — I narrowed my eyes speculatively — either the flower-arranging James or the reasonably nice Joe had a stylish wife who had clearly rejected the idea of breast implants. Was there no end to the mysteries on this block?

It hurt to look at Miracolo, where gawkers were trying to see inside the shuttered window. I watched what appeared to be

Main Liners stop at my door. They looked like people about the right age to know their way around a true antipasto. They also looked like people who might actually have heard of Eve Angelotta before the Incident of October 23, 2009. But the yellow-and-black tape shouting Crime Scene Do Not Cross, strung across the closed door, was just the sort of bad PR that could have lasting effects. I bet they were thinking the head chef probably couldn't tell the difference between a flounder and a blowfish.

I sighed as I watched them move down the street, looking for a substitute. They would doubtless end up at the crêperie around the corner, where the picture of the owner, Eloise Timmler — whose entire former restaurant experience consisted of asking customers if they wanted to up-size their fries and Cokes — was the newest thing on the menu.

As I pushed myself off the low windowsill where Akahana always liked to spend a couple of hours in the evening, someone ran into me, making me stagger.

"Hey! Hi!" It was Mark Metcalf.

The day was suddenly looking up, like maybe I could pull it — stinking just a little — out of the Dumpster that was May 27. High points so far? Bawling freely on Dana

— before I found out about her treachery. Hearing about that sweet good-neighbor discount from the Beck guy. Hiring that piano-playing tiger of mysterious gender, Mrs. Crawford. And now, Mark Metcalf.

Mark was someone I was forever running into. It was as if the cosmos wanted us to, well, do things together. The first time, about a month ago, I ran into him coming out of Starbucks.

He was one of those all-American hotties I secretly yearn for because I feel I owe it to the great, disappearing American cowboy. Like a public service, even. The Marlboro Man without the silly hat or the cigarettes. One of those men who are born tan. Green eyes that, yes, twinkled. Close-cut hair, because who needs long hair when you've got a chin that says you know what you're doing, and lips that say they'll kiss you up right good, missy.

Not that Mark Metcalf and I had gotten to that point.

It would help if our dates weren't always on the run. We had had three of them so far. Drinks always led to food somewhere on the fly, like it was a threesome: Mark, me, and power-walking somewhere while chewing. The good-nights had all ended up strangely nowhere — near a park entrance, a performance just letting out, and a random tree — with me edging away when all I really wanted was to be a flying squirrel splayed against the screen of Mark Metcalf.

I was nothing if not perverse.

Was he gay?

Landon — whom I enlisted to casually walk by one time — declared no.

Was he married?

He once comfortably mentioned an ex-wife out West who was what she termed "an artist in glass" and what he termed achingly neurotic. And that was as much as I got. Mark himself was a day trader whose idea of Italian cuisine involved Chef Boyardee and a can opener.

We had a big laugh.

"So what's going on?" Mark jerked his handsome head toward the other side of the street. I'm pretty sure I had seen Clint Eastwood make the very same move in *High Plains Drifter,* but I think maybe his wool poncho was irritating him.

"Oh, well, murder," I said, waving it away, like it was the second one already this week.

The green eyes twinkled a little less. "Anyone you know?"

"No, it looks like some kind of weird break-in." Technically, I didn't know the dead guy, so I didn't feel like I was lying to

60

someone who could possibly become my husband.

"Anything stolen?"

"Stolen? No." Terrible thought. "Unless you count the Quaker Hills PD making off with the precious Caruso seventy-eight lying under the body." When he looked at me narrowly, I had to explain. "I've got a bunch of opera stuff over there," I said, wondering if it would be the last I'd see of him.

"Cool," he said.

"I've even got the gloves Caruso wore in *Rigoletto* in his first season at the Met."

Mark gasped dramatically. "Not the gloves!"

I gave him a playful little kick in the shin. Just a love tap.

I'd rather have the 78 than the gloves, but Caruso memorabilia doesn't come on the market very often. Caruso collectors are an elusive bunch, worse even than a secret society, since they guard their identities even from each other.

Mark checked his gold watch — he must be good at day trading, whatever that is. "I'd like to see you work sometime, Eve," he said softly, green eyes back to full twinkle mode. In my head, I substituted *work* with *naked.*

"Sure thing, Mark, anytime." Nail him

down. "A week from tonight?" Would the crime scene tape be gone by then?

He leaned in closer. "Nothing sooner?"

"Friday?" I blurted. Never stand in the way of a good-looking man whose only fault is that he wants to see you sooner.

"You're on." He grinned and gave me a peck on the cheek before I knew it was coming and could intercept it with my lips. The man was fast — and elusive. Catching my breath, I got tangled in a swirl of his cologne, something by Serge Lutens that I recognized because I'd snagged a sample card at Saks.

My eyes followed him as he strode up the street. At this rate, the snow would be falling before he and I experienced anything half as cheap and pointless as my onetime adventure with the FedEx man.

My contribution to the Happy Food Potluck at Landon's was a salmon ball.

"Anything, but *anything,* with horseradish is not happy food, Eve," Landon lectured me. "Don't you have sinuses?" I followed him into his granite and Italian tile kitchen, where everything seemed suspended from the high ceiling: a Casablanca fan, a wineglass rack, hooks for his gleaming copper Calphalon cookware.

Landon is a trust fund baby whose six-room condo is in the upscale Innerlight Estates complex overlooking Pensey Park on the south side of town. Maria Pia's younger son, Dom Angelotta, made a fortune in plumbing supplies, which pretty much offset her pique when he announced he was not going to work in the family business. Landon is his only child.

And Landon is the greatest art hag I have ever met. If there's a gallery opening anywhere in the borough of Manhattan, Landon is there with a bottle of Giacomo Conterno Barolo Riserva Monfortino for the owner. He also likes small dance companies and dignified poetry readings.

Four of Miracolo's "human resources" were collected on the leather sofas in the living room, eating happy appetizers, which turned out to be edamame dumplings and caramelized onion Brie *en croute*. Apparently the dumplings and Brie didn't cut it with Landon's handsome tabby cat, Vaughn, who was stretched out on his back pretending to be asleep.

Gathered were Choo Choo, Paulette, Jonathan, and the treacherous Dana, all stakeholders. Paulette Coniglio was one of my father's former lady friends, who had waitressed all her life and still needed a paycheck. I liked her. Jonathan Bolger was still in a closet that appeared to be painted shut, but he was an excellent sommelier, and Landon had hopes.

"Vera will get here when she can," Choo Choo explained, balancing a strangely empty plate on his lap. "She's taking her brother to an AA meeting." We all knew she had finally talked him into going. Red-headed Vera Tyndall was a little younger than my thirty-two, putting herself through Temple University part-time, taking care of her brother, and an all-around good egg. The kind of person you can totally trust with your goldfish and house plants. And she actually liked Maria Pia, who was as difficult as she could be charming.

Landon brought me a plate and a big glass of red wine, probably not from a bottle of the Giacomo Conterno. "And poor, dear Alma will be late, too. She's got her grief support group until eight." Alma Toscano was a hard-luck friend of my grandmother's. When her husband killed himself two years ago, Alma underwent what Maria Pia called a "circumstance revision" — read: she fell on hard times and came to work at Miracolo. She kept going to the support group because they had all bonded, so now it was something social, only without having to learn Mah Jongg.

Working at Miracolo was an answer to grief, tuition, habit, empty nests, man trouble, underemployment, and performance dreams, since both the food and the company were wonderful.

I was chewing an edamame dumpling, waiting for the bliss to happen, when Dana spread a wide smile all around, then folded her hands and turned to me. "So," she said conspiratorially, "tell us what we can do to help."

"Well, Dana," I said, touching a gold cocktail napkin to the lips I was saving for Mark Metcalf, "first, you can tell me why you talked Reginald Jolly out of my spare key."

I expected to hear Dana's sudden intake of breath.

I didn't expect Choo Choo's, Paulette's, Jonathan's, and Landon's, as well.

Something was afoot.

Something not even Brie *en croute* could make okay.

"Well?" I demanded.

Dana clicked her tongue. "Oh, that faithless man!"

The rest of them looked like fourteen-year-olds called out for missing curfew.

"Staff?" I said with cool menace in my voice.

Landon started wringing his hands. "It was a surprise for you, that's all."

So they were all in on it. I actually said, "*Et tu,* Landon?"

"Hear us out," put in Choo Choo. "Next week is June second, and you know what that means: Festa della Repubblica."

"When Italians voted to end the monarchy," piped up Paulette.

"At the end of World War Two —"

"Which made Italy a republic."

"We've been meeting in the mornings," Jonathan explained, "so we could go through the routine."

Landon looked at him with adoration.

"What routine?" I didn't like the sound of this.

Paulette, who had to be close to sixty, actually said, "We didn't want to get out there and suck."

This was getting worse and worse. "At what?" I barked.

They all started talking at once. "The tarantella!" They all looked at me earnestly, their voices tumbling together. What I could make out was anxiety about time running out, reputations to uphold, harder than they thought, spectators, bunions, local TV, and pride. The phrase *dance from hell* was muttered a few times.

When the last one wound down, saying something softly about how they thought I'd be proud, I closed my eyes for a minute, letting them stew, and finally said, "Tell me you're not taking it to the streets."

Choo Choo held up a hand. "Strictly inside. One performance." For a maximal kind of guy, Choo Choo could make the Four Horsemen of the Apocalypse sound like little kids in pony carts.

"But at the height of the dinner rush!" Landon exulted.

Choo Choo shot him a look.

"Okay, okay," I relented. "But I never want you to pull a stunt like this again."

If I could have grounded them, I would have.

Still, they looked contrite.

I sighed. "At least it was just the one key."

I saw a quick, calculating look cross Jonathan's face. He and Dana studied their plates, while Paulette trailed her fingers along the black and brown spots on the cat's belly. Choo Choo tugged at his lower lip and Landon sprang up, brightly announcing that dinner was served.

My head started to throb. "Tell me it's just the one key."

Then Dana had to admit they couldn't all practice on the same mornings, so she had — here she coughed into her hand — copies made.

Once we sorted out who had made copies from their copies, it turned out that all seven tarantella dancers had keys to the Miracolo Italian Restaurant and before-hours rehearsal space. All five of them experienced a temporary lull in appetite when I mentioned, in a wickedly casual way, that now I'd have to report to detectives Ted and Sally that any one of the waitstaff could have been inside the restaurant with the dear departed Arlen Mather.

Although I was hoping for more mileage out of this scare, they were a resilient group who suddenly remembered the purpose of the potluck and worked out a game plan they named Operation Free Maria Pia.

When I pointed out she wasn't in jail, Choo Choo snorted, and Dana drawled, "Well, not yet, darling." Three of them put themselves on neighborhood crawl duty — questioning the shopkeepers on Market Square to see if they had seen or heard anything of interest — and the other two went on background check duty, which meant digging up whatever they could about Mather.

It sounded like a good plan. One they wouldn't have to scheme or trespass anywhere to do.

I looked at them through my raised wineglass. They were my world at Miracolo. My surprise Festa della Repubblica tarantella dancers. I must confess, I got misty.

5

Wednesday

Maria Pia Angelotta, retired chef, owner of Miracolo, potential murder suspect, and Genovese dragon, stood motionless in the center of her high-end, All-Clad-studded kitchen. She seemed lost in a troubling daydream, holding an espresso maker in one hand. Her front door is never locked — a matter of some alarm for Choo Choo, Landon, and me — so she didn't hear me when I greeted her from the arched kitchen doorway.

"Hi, Nonna."

She turned a look of mild interest toward me, taking in my Ann Taylor black twill capris. "Perhaps your legs are not your best feature," she mused.

Not my best feature, indeed! "I'm a dancer."

"Dancers dance."

"Unless they have to work in the family

70

salt mine," I threw out.

"Which keeps them *all* in pants, you should only remember."

Had I come to the end of the Angelotta il-logic thread? The point in these exercises is simply to utter something, no matter how inane. Last man talking, and all that. Whenever I get into one of these conversations with Nonna, I have a full understanding of what happened to the Roman Empire: they finally heard themselves.

When she swung around to me and slumped, I realized how stiffly she'd been holding herself. My seventy-six-year-old nonna was still kind of a dish, what with her masses of springy salt-and-pepper hair, her fine, high cheekbones set in a broad face that could handle every one of those wrinkles, and a nose with the kind of nostrils even money can't buy.

There wasn't a hue on Landon's color wheel that didn't look all the better for simply being near Maria Pia's face. This was a difficult truth when I hit puberty and all the boys I was interested in hung around hoping to get a glimpse of my grandmother in her short black-and-red kimono. It's one thing to look like leftover polenta compared to a dance squad babe who's your age; it's another thing altogether to be outdone by your granny.

"Darling," she cried, as if she had just seen me for the first time. Clamping her hands on my shoulders, Maria Pia steered me over to the wood-and-chrome stools that stood around the S-shaped island in the middle of her kitchen.

We sat.

Nonna was dressed in a pale pink satin robe and matching peep-toe slippers. Her toenails were polished gold. "Tell me," she said, searching my face for some kind of breakdown she could use as a jumping-off point for her own. She'd been in a culinary dry spell for a while, which I contend explains the likes of Arlen Mather. Whenever she wasn't cooking well, she was at risk of a romance with an unsuitable man.

"Didn't the police give you the details?"

"Only that Arlen was . . . attacked." Her lower lip actually quivered and she looked at me for confirmation.

"Well, bludgeoned." Spare the image, spoil the grandmother, I always say.

Her eyes went wide. "A head wound?"

"Oh, yes." With all the sag of my first panettone, the sweet holiday bread.

" 'Wound' always sounds so . . . fixable, don't you think?"

"Well, not when 'fatal' comes in front of

72

it. Believe me, Arlen has eaten his last *risotto alla milanese.*"

I scanned my grandmother's still-beautiful face, certain she was hungering for more, well, description. And when I realized she knew there was no way she could outright ask for it without appearing heartless or — better word — ghoulish, I felt strangely uplifted. "The question, of course, is who killed him."

She looked at me, wide-eyed. "Obviously, *cara.*"

"And how he got inside the restaurant."

"To breathe his last." Shaking our heads, we looked away from each other, pondering for a lengthy nanosecond the cruelty of a world that contains such things as murder and meatballs.

Maria Pia's hands slid through the voluptuous tangle of her hair and she nodded. "Yes, how he got inside Miracolo. I imagine that's what the police want to know." We sat there companionably while she poured me an espresso, slipping a crescent of lemon rind onto my saucer. "Which is why," she said, sitting up straight, "I'll have to tell them the truth."

The hairs on my arms went on high alert. "The truth?"

She licked her lips, a stalling tactic I knew

73

well. Then she finally lifted her hands in bewilderment. "I let Arlen into Miracolo that morning."

Was the sudden, end-of-the-world clanging only in my head?

"Why?" I finally got out.

"He wanted a look at the opera — *come si dice?* — stuff." Suddenly she grinned at me, like this was a winning piece of information. Something I had in common with the flattened boyfriend.

My mouth was hanging open. "You left him there?"

"You don't have to call Children's Services on me, Eve. He was a grown man."

And nothing bad ever happens to grown men. "So you just dropped him off?"

"I was on my way . . . to the mall." Why did I feel like she was making it up as she went along? "The dress I'm wearing for Festa della Repubblica? The alterations are done —"

"Saks?" Sound casual.

"Ma certo." An elegant shoulder lift.

Now I could check her alibi.

"So you just let him in to look over my stuff? Couldn't he do that during normal business hours?" This was smelling like the shipment of sea bass we got last week.

"I didn't think you'd mind. Besides, what

harm would come of it?" She gave me a pained look. "Arlen was a perfectly lovely, respectable —"

"Old soul."

"Exactly." She sighed. "I gave somebody at the *Courier Times* a photo of Arlen and me at the Philadelphia Food and Wine Festival. He was wearing a red ascot" — she bit her lip — "and looked very handsome. I hope I get the photo back."

This from a woman who doesn't own a single photo album.

I asked, "Did you see anyone hanging around?" Say, an entire waitstaff practicing the tarantella?

She cocked her head. "Where?"

"At Miracolo, the morning you dropped Arlen off." I gazed at her over my demitasse.

"There were plenty of people around, Eve." She was fixedly sketching circles in the sunlight on the granite countertop. "But no one in particular."

I dropped my spoon noisily into my saucer. "I know about the tarantella, Nonna," I said in a tone that sounded like I was accusing her of cheating on me.

"Oh, you, you, you, you know so much." With her chin high, she blurted, "He said he'd leave the place exactly the way he found it."

"Oops."

"Sometimes you are really too sarcastic," she told me. "Have a biscotto." Like it was an antidote. One manicured hand pushed the plate of her special pistachio biscotti toward me. Even when she was in a culinary dry spell, my nonna could crank out the pistachio biscotti.

I chose one and took my time studying it. "Why did he take down the shadow box with the Caruso seventy-eight?"

"Did he? Maybe he forgot his glasses." She gave me a typical dramatic shrug, but my Crap Detector started dinging when she didn't look me in the eye. "And I'm pretty sure I told him he could take things out of those silly little show boxes —"

"Shadow boxes, Nonna."

"— to see things up close, as long as he put them back."

My head felt like slow-drying cement. I tried to picture the scene around the corpse, but couldn't. Except for the Caruso 78 and the busted shadow box kicked into the corner. What else had I missed?

We stared each other down so hard, you'd think we were playing Texas Hold 'Em.

I held out my hand.

She looked at me blankly.

"The key, Nonna. Please."

She slammed her hands down on the table. "Whose restaurant is it?"

"Which is why you can appreciate the need for better security," I retorted. "I'll let you in any time you have a good reason."

She glared at me. "You act like you own the place."

"*One* of us should."

"Honestly, Eve, one little mistake —"

"Nonna, please. You know I love you."

"What if you're lying passed out on the floor? Who's going to let in the *paramedici*?"

Oh, for God's sake. "I'll take my chances."

Her eyes narrowed and her voice dropped to a dramatic whisper. "What if it's Landon lying passed out on the floor?"

Low. Really low. I actually gasped and she pressed her advantage, painting the scene. "And Choo Choo is home shaving his head nice and close" — in Maria Pia's view, her grandson's choice to go hairless was akin to my wearing pants — "and you're home wondering what you can wear to ruin your chances."

"Well, if nobody's there," I said, leaning toward her, "who would know if Landon passed out, hey?"

She slammed a hand on her chest and said imperiously, "I am his nonna. I will know."

"All right, Nonna," I said finally. I would

find out why she really let Arlen Mather in to Miracolo. I would find out why he pulled down my Caruso 78. I would find out whether she was indeed on her way to pick up her dress for Festa della Repubblica — or with him, instead. But for now, "Keep the key," I told her, sounding casual. If she thought I'd backed off the key business, she might get reckless.

I asked her, "Was Arlen retired?"

She gave me an innocent look over the rim of her cup. "Semi," she said.

"What did he do?"

"This and that," she offered. And, to clarify: "Here and there."

"You'll have to do better than that with the cops, Nonna."

"Ours," she said grandly, "was a love relationship."

Well, I couldn't go anywhere with that. "Did he leave any stuff here?" Toothbrush? Boxers? Viagra?

She sprang up, raised a finger at me, and flowed out of the kitchen at a pretty good clip. I heard her clip-clop down the hall and up the stairs. Finally she returned with a blue summer-weight blazer over her arm and a Polo Ralph Lauren dopp kit. Luckily, at that moment her landline rang out in the living room and she darted off to answer it.

While she was gone I fished around in Mather's blazer, pulling out a movie stub, a nearly empty packet of Tic Tacs, and — from the breast pocket — a worn blue business card.

Viceroy Vinyl
Your Source for Vintage Opera
   Recordings
Buy · Sell · Appraise
Abel LeMeur
212-765-8302
www.viceroyvinyl.com

With a thrill of discovery, I slipped the business card into my pocket, and then dug around in the kit. Brushes for teeth, nails, and hair. Clippers for nails and nose hair. Mint floss. Three different prescription meds. The only one I recognized was an anticholesterol drug. As I heard Nonna head back toward the kitchen, I hurriedly tapped the names of the other two meds into my phone, then zipped up the kit and set it back on top of the blazer, where she had left it. There's something infinitely sad about going through the personal — very personal — possessions of the newly dead. The dead who got up one morning perfectly healthy and had no idea that Fate was patiently hanging around outside.

When my nonna reappeared, she brushed back some hair with infinite weariness. "It was Choo Choo."

"Nonna," I said, gesturing to Arlen Mather's things, "you'll need to turn these over to the cops."

She staggered back a step. "It feels like poor Arlen is getting lost in all this — this — murder business, do you know what I mean?" She stared for a moment at the pathetic little pile of his things, and then her face fell apart and she started to cry. "He would simply hate all this."

Being the victim and all. I squeezed her shoulder, wishing I were Dana, who could do it better.

She pressed a tissue against her waterproof mascara. "You're thinking I should go to the — the — police place and get it over with."

Maria Pia was just going to have to suck it up and go see Ted and Sally. It would look a whole lot worse if she didn't. "That's a yes, Nonna."

Of course, she shot me a look like I was exiling her in a dugout canoe somewhere deep in the Amazon. "Thank goodness he wasn't shot. They'd want to know if I own a gun."

For the first time in the last twenty hours, I laughed. "Well, if that happened, you'd really have nothing to worry about." If my granny really had a hate on, the worst she'd do is serve somebody butter that she'd left out for a week.

"Well, I don't know why you say that." She seemed offended.

"Oh, that's right," I joked, "I forgot about your nine millimeter Browning handgun."

"Of course I don't own a Browning, Eve." She laughed at the very thought. "You know my gun is a Glock."

I lost no time calling Landon. "Did you know Nonna packs heat?" I slammed myself into my ten-year-old blue Volvo sedan and jammed the key into the ignition.

He was silent for a moment. "Well, does she actually *carry* the, uh, heater?"

I backed out of Nonna's driveway. "Landon, listen to you. 'Heater.' You should try this sexy talk on Jonathan."

"No," he said shortly. "Too much too soon."

I could see his point. "I think Nonna keeps the gun in the drawer with the custard cups. She kept eyeing it while she was telling me that she would never tell me where she keeps it."

81

"The question, of course," said Landon slowly, "is the ammo. I vote for removing it."

"Unanimous."

Landon slipped into his communing-with-the-spirit-world voice. "Check the drawer with the ramekins. Right below the custard cups. That's my guess."

Landon often had flashes of insight into our grandmother's labyrinthine brain. I'd definitely check the ramekin drawer next time. "Is this something we have to worry about at the restaurant?" I had visions of Maria Pia taking out some disgruntled patron who dissed the gnocchi.

As I hit Friends Way, the prettiest boulevard in Quaker Hills, we chewed over whether Maria Pia had a permit for the "heater." We decided she probably didn't. The Glock was likely one of her impulse buys, like the time she bought scuba equipment.

In the short run: snag the ammo. In the long run, we would research plastic Glock look-alikes online and order a replacement for whatever was stashed in the custard cup drawer. She'd probably never miss it.

Then Landon had to go. His assignment for Operation Free Maria Pia consisted of quizzing shopkeepers on the north side of

Market Square for info about suspicious activity in the commercial district the morning of Arlen Mather's murder.

"Be sly, *caro*," I urged him, kind of breathlessly. "Sly."

He tutted at me. "Girlfriend."

"Remember, you're not getting just information. You're getting alibis." Landon was a good choice for that stretch of the district: he was in a bocce league with the owner of Sprouts (Landon designed the team uniform), he hit garage sales with the owner of Pleasure Chest Antiques, and was still on good terms with his former boyfriend Jimi Baker, the locksmith at Baker and Locks.

Of the remaining operatives, Jonathan — who hadn't lived in Quaker Hills for the last ten thousand years and didn't know every citizen's choice in toilet paper — was put on research detail, along with Vera Tyndall. Choo Choo took the shops on the south side of Market Square (he and Reginald's bouncer, Adrian, belonged to the same gym, but Adrian actually went). The charmingly abrasive Paulette got the east side because the group felt those shopkeepers would cave quickly under an Italian steamroller; and I got the leftovers: the Becks, Eloise Timmler from the crêperie around the corner, and Maria Pia herself.

Alma Toscano was assigned to pound the beat on the west side of the square. Landon believed Alma was hoping to entice Sasha Breen, the sleek-like-a-blond-whippet rich-girl owner of Airplane Hangers, into selling her line of hand-decorated shoes, Toscano's Tootsies — "Art for Your Feet!" (or, as the discerning Landon mutters, "Crap for Your Corns!") — at the shop. The hard-luck Alma had apparently cornered the market on felt, feathers, buttons, beads, fabric paint, and glue guns.

I parked the Volvo down the street from Miracolo. Then, pulling out the business card from Arlen's jacket, I put a call in to Abel LeMeur of Viceroy Vinyls. I don't know what I was hoping for, but some insight into Arlen would be a start. How much of a collector of vintage opera recordings was he? And would any possible murder suspects step out of those particular shadows?

The voice that rumbled "Hello" sounded browned by years of cigarettes.

As a cover story, I had decided to shoot for vague with a possibility of money. So I introduced myself and told Abel LeMeur that I was calling about the estate of Arlen Mather. I had discovered a Viceroy Vinyls business card among Mr. Mather's possessions and thought I'd inquire about his appraisal services.

"Mather, you say?" LeMeur sounded a little more alert.

"Right. Arlen Mather."

He told me it must have been a couple of years since Mather came to his shop in Greenwich Village. Bought a rare 1928 recording of Rosa Ponselle singing "Pace, pace mio Dio," and that was it. Only time he ever saw him. Then LeMeur explained his appraisal fees and asked how big Mr. Mather's collection was. This question I sidestepped, shoveling something about how the man had just died and we hadn't gone into many details yet, at which the record seller offered condolences.

"I got the feeling from some things Mather said that he did most of his business with Calladine," said LeMeur.

"Calladine?"

"Geoffrey Calladine in Vancouver. Big, big seller. Calladine's Classics, that's him. Guy's so big he doesn't even have to advertise."

My eyes strayed to the two vehicles that I assumed were unmarked police cars, out in front of Miracolo, but my ears belonged to LeMeur. "Have you got a number for him?" When the guy on the other end sounded cagey, I reassured him that Viceroy Vinyls would handle all our appraisal needs. Mollified, he set down the phone and looked for Calladine's contact info. When he came back on, he rattled off a number with a Vancouver area code. I thanked him and let him go.

Since there was a three-hour time difference, I knew my call to Calladine's Classics would have to wait, so I locked up the Volvo and headed for the restaurant. Crime scene tape still festooned the front door, so I flipped the latch to the stockade fence that rimmed the property and strolled along the flagstone walk that led to the courtyard and outdoor dining area. I picked up an empty sandwich wrapper that had blown over from Sprouts. The last few days had been dry, so any chance at footprints, or whatever else I thought I might find at the scene that the trained professionals had missed, was nil.

I pinched a couple of withered white honeysuckle blooms hanging from the trellis along the long brick wall, then peeked through one of the windows. A couple of CSI guys in paper booties were doing a sweep of the dining room, and a third was dusting for prints on the double doors to the kitchen. I tried to think it through. Was Arlen Mather's killer already inside Miracolo, that morning, waiting for him? Or did he follow him in?

Or — and here, I have to admit, my chest felt rickety — did his killer let him in with her very own key? What could the well-groomed, well-dressed Arlen Mather possibly have said ("You call *this* opera memorabilia?") or done to my pistol-packing nonna to have made her snap? It's not as if he stole her carefully guarded recipe for osso buco (braised veal shanks). It's not as if he's Belladonna Russo, Nonna's culinary archrival, who should stay east of the Delaware River.

As I rounded the building I glanced in the small window to the office, then quickly flattened myself against the wall, hidden by the tumble of honeysuckle spilling over the window frame. Inside the office, standing stock-still between the bookshelves and the closed door leading into the kitchen, was Joe Beck. Clearly hiding.

Why was I always finding this man on my property? Was there some weird trespassing karma going on between us? One day he's violating my compost bin, another he's glommed against my office wall offering up prayers to the gods of likely stories that the CSI guys won't take it into their heads to check out the office.

Which led me to believe that Joe had arrived on the scene before they did.

Now, I may not have a well-thumbed copy of the Pennsylvania Penal Code on one of those bookshelves next to Joe's very nice shoulder, but I was reasonably surprised his morning was including breaking and entering. Was he not what he seemed?

Angry, I stepped in front of the window and waved my arms like I was a castaway and he was a low-flying plane. Finally, he noticed, and then the conversation got interesting.

He pressed his lips together and gave me a wry look.

I thrust my arms at him in a gesture meant to convey something along the lines of *ya-ha?*

He jerked his head toward the closed door. Twice.

I smiled wickedly and folded my hands in plain sight.

He sagged dramatically.

I widened my eyes at him.

He widened his eyes at me.

I gave him a carefully crafted look of disgust and indulgence. Then, with a stony glare, I jabbed a thumb at myself, made a yakking-it-up gesture with my hand, pointed to the CSI team, rippled an eyebrow at the hapless Joe Beck, then shoved a finger at him and showed him two fingers running away. He seemed keen and grateful.

I walked to the back door, limboed under the yellow tape, and let myself into the kitchen, leaving the back door slightly ajar. With a quick glance at the closed door to the office, I noisily stamped my feet and exhaled like I had just made it to Everest base camp. When a couple of unfamiliar heads appeared in the round windows of the double doors, I gave them the full personality.

"Hey! Hi! I'm Eve! This is my place!"

"Listen, this is —"

Skirting the taped body outline on the tiles near my prep table, I motored over to them. "I found something!" I declared, brandishing the crumpled wrapper from Sprouts.

"You can't be in here —"

"Do you think it's important?" I pushed my way into the dining room. "Is it a clue?" Perturbed but curious — like dogs in training wondering when the hell the treats were going to make an appearance — they followed me away from the double doors over to the bar, where they had set their crime scene kits. I gave the team my most riveting expression — which I hoped wasn't coming across as psychopathic — and launched into a tale of my walk around the side of the building, as told by Edgar Allan Poe.

To hear me tell it, the crumpled wrapper was capable of spells, boils, the evil eye, and choking you with a tasteless vegan sandwich. I dropped the offending clue into the gloved palm of one of the team, who thanked me through gritted teeth and reminded me to please not cross the police tape again.

At that moment, I saw Joe stroll past the front windows, giving the wandering Akahana a pat on the back. I suddenly lost interest in the CSI team, mumbled a thanks, and slipped out the back. In the short time it took me to hit the street, he was gone. I stormed two doors up to the florist shop, where the red-and-white Open sign hung lopsidedly on the inside of the door. *You bet you're open.* I was so mad, I felt like I had lockjaw.

Joe was half collapsed against the counter, his head in his hands.

"What were you doing inside my restaurant?" I demanded.

He looked up. "Thanks for getting me out of there."

"You're welcome," I said like I had just granted him an audience with the queen. "But you didn't answer my question." I crossed my arms, taking in his nicely creased charcoal pants and pale pink shirt. A burgundy-and-gray tie was neatly coiled near the register. *Looking good, Beck.* To stay focused, I was going to have to force myself to recall the floral swim trunks.

"Visions of disbarment danced in my head. Since when do CSI teams show up this early?"

This appeared to be rhetorical, so I pressed on. "Did you have a key?" Like half the population of Albania. "Or did a set of lockpicks come with your law degree?"

"The door was open."

"Oh, right." I snorted attractively.

"It was," he said with some energy. "I thought my wedding ring might be in the couch."

Then he fished around in his pants pocket and pulled out a gold band, looking triumphant.

I don't know why it all chose that moment to come crashing down, but it did.

Nonna would be suspected of murder.

I had fallen off the stage of the New Amsterdam Theatre. Only once, but it would feel like every night for the rest of my life.

And I would die manless, hunched like a *strega* over an onion-anchovy sauce.

"Look," I said, my chin quivering, "I want you to stay off my property. Thank you for yesterday with the keyboard and all." I started to back away. "But I don't want to find you climbing out of my compost or hiding in my office or — or — dancing the tarantella in my dining room, okay? You want to come in for a great thank-you meal sometime, once we're back open and my nonna's safe and the only thing my crazy cousin Kayla does" — I glared at him, dialing up the volume — "is . . . her *job,* then fine, you come, and I'll make you and your poor wife a saltimbocca so good, it'll fool you into thinking you're still in love —"

"You're a little late," he said, his mouth twisting. "We've been divorced a few years."

"Well, then," I said grandly, "dinner for one." He was still getting the risotto. "But until that time, stay away from my property. And stay away from me."

If Nonna wants to hire him, *she* can make the phone call.

I didn't know why I was so agitated. Maybe it had something to do with feeling like my life was flying out of control. Or maybe it had something to do with the fact that pink shirts on hot men are strangely sexy.

I turned on my heel and left. Halfway to

the door, I felt a hand slip around my upper arm. "Hey, I'll make you some tea. Come on, Eve, you can't go solving crimes looking like you just committed one yourself —"

"Oh, look who's talking."

He pulled me around to face him. "Look," he said, his hand lingering on my arm. I was hoping it was far enough away from my heart that he didn't feel it pounding. After an indecisive moment when I wondered whether his hand was going to do something more interesting, he finally gave my arm a squeeze and let go. "Just one cup of tea."

"Don't you have someone to go defend, or something?"

He checked his watch and headed toward the workroom. "Not until later."

I followed him into the workroom, which was the heart of the Flowers by Beck operation. The classroom where I'd auditioned Mrs. Crawford had a "public face" polish that was missing here in the back. Aside from two sinks and a threadbare blue-and-green-checked couch, there were large worktables, shelves holding pretty vases of various shapes and sizes, wall-mounted rolls of green florist paper, plenty of wire, and enough Styrofoam to float Venice.

I sat on the couch and hugged my knees, watching Joe pour from the hot water carafe on a two-unit coffeemaker. Into a mug emblazoned with *Failure Is Not an Option — Kennedy Space Center,* he plunked a tea bag, a teaspoon, and a drizzle of honey. Then he handed it to me. "This will set you right up." He patted my back in a *there, there* sort of way.

I sipped what turned out to be chamomile, and eyed my host.

Joe pulled up a chair, swung it around, and sat. We looked at each other for a while, the way I've seen people look when they're standing in front of cubist paintings, then he scratched his head. "I'm sorry we've gotten off to a bad start."

"Me, too, I guess," I mumbled. Graciousness, thy name is Eve.

"Anything new on the murder?" said Joe, his eyes wide with curiosity. The blue was pretty dazzling.

I gave him a shrug. "Maria Pia let the guy into the restaurant, so she may be calling you up about that good-neighbor discount."

Joe leaned back, looking pensive. "Opportunity, then."

I heaved a sigh.

"Motive?"

"Are we really going to do this?" I raised the mug for another soothing sip.

"I think we should."

I felt myself blushing. That last time I had that exact exchange, I ended up in the back office with the FedEx guy. Strangely, it was all I could do not to run a thumb along Joe's cheek to see just how close his shave was.

I shook my head like I was trying to clear a three-beer buzz. "On the motive issue," I said finally, "none known, but she's hiding something."

Joe let that sink in, then he said, "Means?"

I made a vague gesture. "She can swing a mortar with the best of them."

"So where was it?"

"The mortar?"

He nodded. "Where do you keep it? In a cupboard? Out on the counter? Where?"

I dimly got why this was an interesting question. If the mortar and pestle were kept in a cupboard, the killer had to know where to find them — a totally creepy thought, since it let out all the waitstaff, and narrowed the field to those of us who knew how the kitchen worked. After all, if I suddenly needed a tool for stirring the polenta, I automatically knew just where to reach for a flat whisk. But since I hadn't killed Mather, that left Landon, Choo Choo, Li Wei the dishwasher, and Maria Pia.

Not good.

Although . . . that scenario left out the

possibility of premeditation. If the killer had arrived before Mather and had murder in mind, he could have spent an interesting hour browsing the possibilities: knives galore, rolling pins, bread boards, skewers, meat thermometers, and gas ovens. Suddenly the field blew wide open.

I was the happiest I had felt in the last day and a half.

But the more I thought about it, the more convinced I was that the mortar had not been inside a cupboard the night before the murder. I had ground some nutmeg to jazz up my spinach alla piemontese that evening, and I was pretty sure Li Wei hadn't washed it before he had to leave.

No, the black marble mortar and pestle were sitting out overnight on the counter near the prep table. I looked up at Joe, who was waiting patiently. "It was out. The mortar was out."

He said nothing.

I went on: "Which means my grandmother could still have done it."

"Eve, it means anybody could have done it," he said with a smile. "*I* could have done it."

I narrowed my eyes, remembering my assignment in Operation Free Maria Pia. "So where were you that morning?"

"In trial."

I sagged. "Plenty of witnesses?"

He gave me a smile. "Try the county prosecutor. She's the one most likely to remember me. I got the case dismissed."

Well, at least it felt good to eliminate somebody.

"Listen, I know I've been a nuisance. Let me make it up to you," he said, sounding like he'd come up with the answer to the melting polar ice cap.

The chamomile tea with honey had pretty much taken care of it, but Joe didn't know that. "What do you have in mind?" I sat up straight, in negotiating mode . . . and noticed that his dimple appeared even when he wasn't smiling. Feeling suddenly chari-table — or cynical — I had a glimmer into why cases got dismissed.

"I've got contacts. If your cousins don't turn up anything on Mather, then come to me."

"Okay."

He stuck out his hand, like we were strik-ing a deal.

I said fine, and shook.

Holding my hand a couple of seconds too long, he said great.

And just as I was thanking him, the bell of the front door tinkled insistently, and Joe

left to sell some posies for his absent
brother.

6

"Chef Angelotta?" came the deep, nasal voice.

"Yes?" I had just turned onto Callowhill Street, on my way to Full of Crêpe to grill Eloise Timmler, when the call came, and I fumbled at my phone. "Mrs. Crawford?" I guessed.

"Yes. Are you in the neighborhood?"

Which neighborhood? "Of the restaurant?"

A beat. "Of course."

"Just around the corner," I told her. "Why?"

"Meet me out front. I may have some information." And she hung up.

I must admit I felt a little frisson of . . . something. I think fear.

I didn't trust that woman — or man. No matter if she — or he — played like Art Tatum. I turned on my heel and leadenly headed back in the direction of Market

Square. Was it coincidence that Mrs. Bryce Crawford, pianist, showed up within an hour of my discovery of the murder victim on my kitchen floor? Don't they always say killers return to the scene of the crime?

Some information. Was it a trap? In broad daylight? With shoppers and a CSI team milling around? What did my brawny new part-time pianist think I knew? What *did* I know? Besides a toe-curling recipe for cannoli that my bigoted grandmother never let me put on the menu? (The whole Sicilian thing.)

But wait.

I had set up the audition with Mrs. Crawford two days before the murder.

But wait.

That could mean she was a pianist *and* a planner. A premeditating piano-playing planner.

But wait. As I rounded the corner, I saw her waiting for me on the sidewalk outside Miracolo. Today she was dressed in a coral cocktail dress with a Jackie Kennedy veiled pillbox hat and shoes dyed to match. A green clip in the shape of a lizard held back half of her wiry hair. Over her shoulders glittered a light silver crocheted wrap that would send Landon into a tizzy. She was carrying a Florida green clutch and a folded newspaper. Her chin was lifted, and she appeared mysterious and composed as she kept her eyes on a robin flying in and out of a space between the building's gutter and the eave.

I stopped alongside her and asked, "What do you think of Etta James?"

A thinly penciled eyebrow lifted, although her gaze didn't move. "Sadly underrated."

I crossed my arms. "On a par with Ella Fitzgerald?"

"Yes," she said with a veiled look, "but that's not a popular opinion."

It was hard not to like a woman who dolled up that much on a Wednesday morning. Someone who dressed retro without realizing it was retro. Was this the stuff killers are made of?

"So, Mrs. Crawford, what have you got for me?"

She unfolded the newspaper and held it out to me. "Is this the gentleman who expired in your restaurant?"

Two lady shoppers in boiled wool jackets and Hush Puppies gave us a terrified look as they passed.

"You do know it had nothing to do with the food?" I shrilled at Mrs. Crawford — and them.

"Yes, of course."

My eyes swept over the lead story in the Bucks County *Courier Times.* There was the photo of local businesswoman Maria Pia Angelotta and her escort, "murder victim" Arlen Mather. I thought "escort" sounded kind of cheesy. But that was probably less important than the fact that the two festivalgoers looked bleary, as if the wine at the Food and Wine Festival had met way too much with their approval.

The news story didn't have much to add — found dead, suspected foul play (unless, I suppose, Arlen had curled up on the floor for a nap and the mortar had fallen on his skull — repeatedly), persons of interest, ongoing investigation. Nothing much about the man himself — no background, no work history — since the extent of my nonna's helpfulness seemed to end at handing over a picture.

I looked up at Mrs. Crawford, waiting for her to divulge . . . whatever.

"The gentleman was a friend of this Maria Pia?" she asked, her eyes glimmering.

I was thankful she didn't call him an escort. "My grandmother, yes."

She narrowed her eyes at the clouds. "And not much is known about him?"

"Apparently not."

She met my eyes. "I believe I may have

seen him before."

Aha! "Where?" I blurted. Following up astutely with, "When?"

She looked at me squarely. "I played a gig about eight months ago. He was there, this Arlen" — she glanced at the newspaper — "Mather, although I never heard the name. I played during the champagne reception and before the auction began."

My heart rate picked up. "What was it?"

"It was a fund-raiser at the Academy of Music, on Broad Street. For the Opera Company of Philadelphia."

So the mysterious Mr. Mather attended opera fund-raisers. No, Mrs. Crawford had no recollection whether he bid on anything during the auction. But he was wearing a tuxedo and his daughter wore a mixed strand of pearls and a feathered boa that proved more tasteful than one would think.

His daughter?

After telling Mrs. Crawford I'd call her about her start date once the police let us open, she handed me the *Courier Times* and clicked back up the street in her coral pumps.

I had just speed-dialed Nonna when the Culiform Supply panel truck pulled to a stop at the curb. Our uniform service. Hell, I forgot to head *them* off at the pass. So I hung up on Nonna when I heard, *"Pronto?"* and dialed the carpet cleaners, the linen service, and the food wholesalers. Between calls, I explained to the Culiform Supply driver — the bodybuilding Carly, according to her name pin and wingspan — that homicide had temporarily dampened our need for restaurant wear. Much paperwork and many sighs ensued.

While Carly fumed and blustered, several neighbors wanted updates.

Mr. von Veltheim, the baker, presented me with some complimentary kugelhopf, which I accepted.

Sasha Breen, looking especially whippet-like, said she heard it was a mob hit. From her lips, it sounded like foreplay. I assured her that unless the mob's preferred method of extinction these days was kitchenware, she had nothing to worry about.

Akahana mentioned that Emperor Hirohito was an excellent ballroom dancer.

Weird Edgar from the Quaker Hills Service Department unloaded the trash can in front of Sprouts, and said he moonlights as a bodily fluids cleanup guy. Reasonable rates. He actually handed me a business card that said Gross-B-Gone, No Guts, No Gory.

A ponytailed fourth-grader pulling a pink

backpack on wheels told me her daddy said my granny was going to fry. At that, I wished I'd paid more attention to Nonna whenever she worked up a good evil eye. And, really, I started to say something highroad, like the only thing my "granny" fries is heavenly *gnocchi fritti,* and such a nice little girl as she was should stop by sometime for one.

But what came out was that her daddy was an ignoramus, and that she should get her Little Debbie Cosmic-Brownies-loving butt out of there before I called the school to report her as a truant. So she did.

Cradling the kugelhopf, I crossed the street to Providence Park at the center of the commercial district, waving at Dana and Vera, who were coming toward me from the eastern end of the park. While I melted onto a park bench and waited for them, pondering the clues about Arlen Mather's love of opera, I called Maria Pia. "Did Arlen have a daughter?"

"A — daughter? Where did you hear this?"

"From Mrs. Crawford, our new pianist."

"We have a pianist?"

"Yes. Three nights a week to start."

"Italian?"

"Actually, hard to say." Among other things . . . "But I think you'll like . . . her."

Nonna gave me one of her florid grunts that covers everything from *The pope just got rid of another saint* to *Customers will break their teeth on this ravioli dough.* "About this daughter . . ." she said languidly, "I know nothing. Such a person never came up."

She asked where this pianist got the information and I mentioned the fundraiser for the Opera Company of Philadelphia eight months ago. So — I pointed out — not only did Arlen Mather have a daughter, he may have had some interest in Miracolo's opera memorabilia.

She said that just because he died on the great Caruso, it didn't mean he loved him. As I tried to make sense of her point, she started to rev up with alternatives to the daughter theory — it could have been a stranger, an opera singer, an escort.

Then Dana and Vera were approaching.

"Gotta go, Nonna —"

"You know, come to think of it, my poor Arlen was dating someone when he met me."

That stopped me in my tracks. "Wait, what?"

Maria Pia went all airy on me. "Just someone. Of course," she purred, "he broke it off."

■ ■ ■ ■

Stranger, opera singer, escort, girlfriend.

Ah, the possibilities. I wondered whether Sally the detective had heard about the female with the pearls and feathered boa.

"Chérie!" Dana kissed me on both cheeks, then chafed my upper arms as if trying to start a fire. She had clearly slipped back into one of her French phases, so we could expect a staggering amount of Edith Piaf during her late-night gig at the restaurant. Her cork platform heels jacked her up about four inches in her beige stretchy leggings, and the bat-wing tunic top sported a stained-glass design. There was just something irrepressible about her that I liked.

"Hey, Dana. Vera."

Vera was wearing a white hoodie and jeans. No manicure, ever, and no jewelry today, just a tightly rolled orange bandana tied like a headband in her mass of red hair. When Dana explained that she had met with Vera to give her some guidance about her investigative role, Vera shot me a tolerant look.

I couldn't resist. "So, what's your own part in the operation, Dana?"

"Coordinator," she said serenely, reminding me of Maria Pia whenever she has to explain why she keeps her recipe for osso bucco in a safe deposit box at the local Wells Fargo Bank.

We stood in a tight little group, taking in the Wednesday-morning crowd on Market Square. What had started out as weakly sunny was now clouding over. "Have the cops taken your statements?" I asked them, watching Weird Edgar round the corner in his red Service Department truck mounted with a megaroll of white trash bags.

"Not yet," said Vera. "I'm supposed to stop in sometime today."

"Dana?"

"Oh, yes," she said with a smile, "I went to the station house first thing yesterday."

"So how was it?" I shifted my weight.

She laughed, tucking her chin-length black hair behind her ears. "I've been asked tougher questions when I get my driver's license renewed." The stained-glass bat wings fluttered. "Name, address, occupation —"

"Alibi," I threw in.

"Of course! I was working at the office that morning. There's always lots to do."

I nodded. Though Dana sings for us four nights a week, mainly she manages her husband's office — Cahill Enterprises — on the second floor of the Ashbridge Building, the redbrick colonial that dominated the eastern end of our Quaker Hills commercial district. Dana Cahill née Mahoney had hit the husband jackpot ten years ago when local businessman Patrick Cowan Cahill fell for her.

He had great hair, great skills, and great taste in everything except shoes and — excluding Dana — women. We'd dated once, but the tassel loafers were a deal breaker for me. And my double-pierced right earlobe was a deal breaker for him. We had a good laugh over it. All of Quaker Hills had suffered through his fling with the alcoholic mud wrestler, his affair with the strident tattoo artist, and his engagement to the hysterical single mom with three small boys.

So, when he married Dana Mahoney, word went out around town that she wasn't an embarrassment or a lunatic and that chances were really pretty good that she wouldn't put undue strain on Quaker Hills's mental health resources.

I felt a pang as Dana made off with the agreeable Vera, promising to check in later. Just as I was wondering whether Vera would become Danacized, which would lead to aberrations such as gold lamé slides worn with herringbone pants, my phone rang. It was Landon telling me he was just walking into the Quaker Hills Police Department with Nonna, who, apparently, was channeling Anne Boleyn in that final walk across the grassy yard at the Tower of London toward the guy in the black hood.

Over on Callowhill Street, I made it into Full of Crêpe (the place's real name is Le Chien Rouge, but I believe in truth in advertising) before the downpour. About a dozen ladies who brunch were ogling the crêpe selections on the daily board over the open kitchen. The choices on Wednesday, May 28, included crêpes with raspberry glop, chocolate sludge, or apple pecan gruel. Full of Crêpe had opened last October, debuting a pumpkin purée crêpe that become strangely popular with the tourists coming out from Philly for the fall colors (since Philly doesn't have trees).

Apparently the entrepreneurial Eloise had emigrated from Wilkes-Barre, where she had managed a Payless shoe store. Before that, she had assistant-managed a Family Dollar store. And sometime before that came her stint with french fries. This vast experience led to Eloise's wanting to open her own "crêpe place" — from Eloise's lips, *crêpe* rhymes with *grape* — in the tourist-magnet of Quaker Hills. So she opened Le Chien Rouge, moved her personal belongings into the apartment over the shop, and still had a PODS storage unit out front in the driveway.

A waitress with hair like Margaret Thatcher preened around the room dressed in Eloise's version of a French folk costume — starchy white sashes and a "hat" that looked like a colors-of-the-French-flag version of Burger King's large fries container. Eloise was visible in the open kitchen, her sandy-colored hair pulled back in a clip, her challenging orthodontics now down to a single wire across her top teeth.

"Hi, Eve," Eloise called out. I watched her ladle something that looked like cherry-colored tar over a couple of crêpes. Amazingly, the music floating through the crêperie was a disco version of "La Marseillaise." The whole operation was cheesier than Maria Pia's *fonduta*.

I think what killed me was how popular the place was. We weren't really competitors, but what made me so jealous was that she got to have this success without a Maria Pia arguing with her over the daily specials or dissing her wardrobe.

"So, Eloise, tell me," I said, sauntering

around the counter. I have to admit, I was just going through the motions. Her joint was a block and a half away from Miracolo; what were the chances she saw anybody skulking into the restaurant behind Arlen Mather? Huh — about as small as Maria Pia giving me the go-ahead to make cannoli at Miracolo. "You heard about the, uh, murder?"

"Yeah," she looked up at me from slathering the cherry-colored topping around the crêpes, "and you found the guy, right?"

"That'd be me," I admitted. "One of my luckier breaks."

"Like falling off a stage," she bleated.

There was nothing I could do about my burning cheeks, but I made a mental note of Eloise's health code violations in her kitchen: open garbage can, unrinsed plates in the open dishwasher, fruit sauces in unlabeled mason jars, and an unnecessary person (me) in the food prep area. I smiled. "See anybody suspicious outside my place that morning?"

"You mean, aside from your grandmother?"

Happily, I had the Health Department on my speed dial. I cocked my head at this woman who will never know what hit her when they descend. "Yes, aside from my grandmother." I even smiled. And it wasn't fake.

She flung the plate on the counter and hit the bell. "Nope, nobody."

"But you were in sight of Miracolo?"

"Yep." She bared her teeth at me in the Eloise version of a smile. "I got a parking spot right on Market Square. How often does that happen, right?"

This from a woman who could park in her own driveway, if she finished moving in and got the PODS unit out of the way. "What time was that, Eloise?"

She thought for a moment. "Must have been nine twenty–ish." Then she hammered the bell two more times. "Babette!" she hollered at the sole waitress, a woman I knew for a fact was named Dora.

"So you saw Maria Pia drop the man off in front of Miracolo —"

"Well, not exactly."

"So," I said slowly, trying to get the story straight, "you *didn't* see her drop him off?"

Eloise grabbed a dirty apron from a stool and wiped her hands on it, violation number 5. "She didn't drop him off."

But Maria Pia admitted to dropping him off. Was she covering for somebody? Was that it? "What are you saying? Wasn't she there?" I couldn't make sense of it.

"Oh, yeah, she was there, all right. She pulled up, the old guy got out and let himself into the restaurant, and she parked the car."

"What!"

"He went in, but so did she." She kept wiping her hands, but all I could hear were the sounds of the pouring rain and the chatter of the customers. "Eve, face it, kid, your grandmother followed him inside."

Eloise sent me out into the rain with a complimentary cherry crêpe. My brain felt like a snow globe, all water and fake, excitable white stuff. As I automatically headed in the direction of Market Square, I downed Eloise's freebie. Glop never tasted so good. Suddenly I felt strangely attached to Full of Crêpe — it was a warm and good place full of attempts at Frenchness and health code violations that really weren't very important, a place where, yes, the floor might be dirty, but people don't end up dead on it. An altogether fine establishment.

I let myself into the Volvo and ratcheted the seat back. A quick call to Directory Assistance gave me the number to Saks. When I got a silky woman's voice, who murmured, "Personal Shopping," I told her who I was, and that I wanted to check on whether my grandmother had picked up her altered dress, so I didn't have to run down there myself.

I waited with my eyes closed while she checked. And it was no real surprise to me when the murmuring Saks lady got back on the line, and told me she was sorry she couldn't save me a trip. Because Maria Pia Angelotta's dress was still there.

It wouldn't be cool to call Landon while he was with Nonna at the Quaker Hills Police Department. Sooner or later Ted and Sally would get around to Eloise Timmler, so all I wanted to do was investigate like I was doing one of the time challenges on Top Chef until that moment came. That was all I knew.

Maria Pia had never appeared as mysterious to me as she did at that moment in my Volvo sanctuary, waiting out the rain. My mind was skittering all over the place. That silly, useless catchphrase, *there has to be a reasonable explanation,* kept colliding with some cannier, less evolved place in my brain that kept repeating just one primal suggestion: *damage control, damage control, damage control.*

Whenever the sensible Eve piped up with good questions about why Maria Pia was lying her ass off, the rest of me just wanted another of Eloise's orgasmic cherry crêpes. Finally, I stared long enough through the rain cascading down the windshield that an important piece of information registered: the black-and-yellow Police Line Do Not Cross tape was . . . gone. Gone!

Grabbing my stuff, I flung myself out of the Volvo and darted to the front door. Inside the restaurant, I sank teary-eyed against the closed door.

No traces of anything out of the ordinary. Of cops or killers or Arlen Mather's final steps.

Taking a deep breath, I looked around the dining room. The tables, the piano, the shadow boxes that hadn't come down from the wall, all looked inexpressibly dear to me. I loved the rough brick walls, the black glossy trim on the windows, the sheer curtains as light as a dragonfly's wings.

I needed one simple task. That's all I wanted.

Pay the rent. There you go.

I walked through the kitchen, not looking at the place where Arlen had hit the floor. In the office, where Joe Beck had begun his day feeling up my leather couch and avoiding the CSI team, I sat at the desk, pulled out the checkbook, and made out the June rent check to Mar-Jo Properties. I might not have any answers for my nonna's behavior, but this much I knew: tomorrow, Miracolo reopens.

Before I tackled all the calls I needed to make to get us up and running again, I realized it was now respectable business hours out on the West Coast, so I called Calladine's Classics in Vancouver. It went right to voice mail. "Calladine," came a voice that sounded like a reference librarian you've just roused from poring over a bibliography on medieval undergarments. "Leave a message."

Frustrated, I gave him my name, number, and something about an estate collection. I purposely didn't mention Arlen's name since I didn't know where that relationship stood. First, get him on the phone, then feel him out about the murder victim.

I slipped the rent check in my pocket, where I felt something else, and pulled out Weird Edgar's Gross-B-Gone business card. Add him to the call list. I might even have to have him come a couple of times before I'd believe our kitchen floor has no trace of Arlen. Then I ducked out the back door and headed up Market Square to the Ashbridge Building on the east end, where the Mar-Jo offices were located. The rain was letting up, and shoppers were stepping back out into the square.

Absently fingering the two earrings in my right earlobe, I climbed the stairs to the second floor, ducking into the sprawling office space of Cahill Enterprises. Patrick was just coming through his glass-enclosed executive office, sleek leather briefcase in hand. "Eve!" He seemed so genuinely happy to see me, I found myself wishing I could offer him a couple of my secret-recipe cannoli.

White shirt, khaki pants, blue-and-gold-striped tie. Very Patrick.

He gave me a quick kiss on only one cheek, apparently unaffected by Dana's return to Frenchness.

I gestured at his shoes: cordovan-colored tassel loafers.

He laughed, then pointed, with a shudder, to my double-pierced ear.

"Lucky thing," I said, crossing my arms.

"You're telling me," he said with a smile.

"If you wore Timberlines and I wore pearls . . ." I shook my head.

Patrick nodded in agreement. "There's no telling how much trouble we would have gotten into."

"You never would have met Dana," I pointed out to him.

"And you never would have met . . . well
—" He seemed stumped.

"— any number of forgettable men," I
finished. Did that sound too pathetic? Too
much like a flash mob?

Patrick leaned against an empty desk. He
was a Type A personality who was either
unusually low-key — in order to hear him,
you had to lean in pretty close — or headed
for a breakdown. I was undecided which.
So, because he and I were friends, I checked
in with him every so often just to gauge how
life was going.

"Aside from the murder, Eve, how are
things down the street?"

"The crime scene techs just left," I told
him, "so tomorrow we'll open for dinner."

He nodded. "Dana was worried that if the
restaurant stayed closed for a long time, she
wouldn't be in good voice."

"Oh, no worries there, Patrick," I said
ambiguously. Which led very suavely to my
next question. "Besides, she's always got
Cahill Enterprises. She worked yesterday
morning, right?"

"That she did," he confirmed softly. "She
rolled in around eleven thirty."

11:30?

Hardly morning.

He went on, "She said she had some

119

things to take care of before showing up here."

Some things to take care of?

I faked my way through the conversation with Patrick while trying to remember exactly what Dana had told me. *I was working at the office that morning.* She deliberately made it sound like she was there from 9 a.m. until noon. Only she wasn't. There were more than two hours unaccounted for. Which meant Dana had deceived me about the morning of Arlen Mather's murder.

7

It's truly tough when you realize you're the sort of person your friends and family lie to and sneak around. I mean, not everybody I know is Italian, so why were they all behaving that way? What explained Dana? And not, for once, in a big existential way? While I watched Jimi Baker in his black muscle shirt and Eagles cap replace the lock on Miracolo's front door, I pondered the problem.

From the kitchen came the sloshing sounds of Weird Edgar, who had happily given up his lunch hour to provide Gross-B-Gone services. I was a little taken aback when he told me I qualified for his "buy one, get one half price" promotion, "because you never know what unwanted bodily fluids life's gonna deposit on you." Even as he pressed the coupon into my hand, I wondered just how much human effluence he thought I was good for. By the time he got around to buffing the floor, I was chained to the office desk phoning our suppliers, trying to hear them over the sounds of Weird Edgar, who you'd swear was busting broncos.

Landon called to report that our nonna had held up very well with the cops. She shoveled them the line about how she had dropped off Arlen at Miracolo to look at the opera memorabilia, and they hadn't asked her much else. Now Landon was taking her to lunch, where they'd happily gab about who was hotter, Al Pacino or Andy Garcia.

Choo Choo called to say he had a little something to show me. I found myself wondering whether he could use the coupon from Weird Edgar.

When I called Kayla to tell her to deliver the usual order tomorrow, she said, "Goody gumdrops." Now, some people might think that was sarcasm. I, on the other hand, knew it was.

Alma checked in. She had gotten a free sample at Starbucks, entered a sweepstakes at the Prudential Real Estate office, and talked the shoe repair guy into putting a pair of Toscano's Tootsies in his window. When I pressed her about her mission, she said nobody had seen a thing outside the restaurant yesterday morning. She still had plenty of shopkeepers to question, but she didn't want to miss *Judge Judy* and had to get back to her apartment.

It's so hard to get good free help these days.

Then Paulette shrilled at me over the phone that she thought the blind bookstore owner was shifty, and the old lady owner of the card shop was holding out on her, never mind the wheelchair, but she was pretty sure she was close to breaking the Korean kid at the dry cleaner's. Paulette's pop, CoCo Coniglio, hadn't been a New York city police detective for nothing, never mind the charges that ended his career. "The *bistecca* doesn't fall far from the *vacca*, hey?" Leaving me to wonder whether she had actually said the steak doesn't fall far from the cow, the redoubtable Paulette hung up. Off, I supposed, to finish breaking the dry-cleaner kid.

If the ship goes down, I want Paulette in my lifeboat. She'd scoop up fish with her bare hands, organize the rowing, and toss complainers overboard. Why she wasn't enough to keep Jock — my disappearing father — in town was a mystery along the lines of how Belladonna Russo's recipe for tiramisu kept winning year after year at the Bella Cucina Cooking Competition, when you can tell she uses prepackaged ladyfingers. Just don't bring it up to Nonna, who plots how to catch her rival in the act of ripping open the Stella D'oro plastic package. *That cheat! That shortcut-taker! That strega!*

I was glad to see the last of Weird Edgar, who crammed my check into his pocket and had to make three trips to his truck to get all the equipment out of my kitchen. Which, I have to admit, looked very nice. Back to its pre-homicide spit and polish. Now I could happily sashay around the Miracolo kitchen, rearranging utensils, canisters, and hanging pans.

My most rebellious move consisted of dragging the prep table noisily over the exact spot where Arlen Mather had breathed his last. But then everything looked crooked. Nothing looked right. Would Landon and Li Wei the dishwasher and I just be bumping into each other now? Would my food — I could hardly say the word — suffer? Why couldn't Arlen Mather have fallen parallel to the table, instead of perpendicular? Was I really this neurotic? No wonder my friends and family lied their patooties off to me.

At that moment my ragtime ringtone started warbling. "Hello?" I recognized the number.

"Geoffrey Calladine," came a soft, precise voice that sounded like it had moved on to bibliographies on Renaissance chamber pots.

Expecting a gabfest on the opera-recording buying habits of Arlen Mather, I headed into the office. I trotted out my line about looking into collection appraisals, which was met with a tepid hum from Geoffrey Calladine.

When I mentioned Arlen Mather, Calladine said, "Who?"

"Arlen Mather," I repeated slowly. "It's his collection I'm calling about. I understand he's done a fair amount of business with you?"

"You've been misinformed."

Huh? The Greenwich Village seller, LeMeur, had no reason to string me along.

"This is the first I've heard his name, Ms. Angelotta," said my man in Vancouver. "I'm sorry to disappoint you, but I didn't know him."

I had to figure what this guy was hiding, so I said a fast good-bye. *What was going on?* Was this Geoffrey Calladine running some kind of shady business, and had my nonna's boyfriend been part of it somehow? I had called a Vancouver cell phone number, but that didn't mean Calladine was actually in Vancouver. Could he be . . . here in Quaker Hills? I walked just a little weak-kneed back into my kitchen, pretty much on course for freaking myself out altogether.

Which was when I saw Dana.

Jimi Baker was also replacing the lock on the back door, and when he got a call he'd wandered off to the side of the restaurant, leaving the door wide open. I stepped outside to pick up a screwdriver he'd dropped, and as I straightened back up, I spotted Dana in a third-story window, two doors up from the restaurant. Right next door to us, on the other side of the Miracolo fence, was The Bead Hive, a bead shop in a freestanding, two-story building like ours. But next to The Bead Hive was the narrow, three-story Logan Building, with Sprouts at street level. But I'd never thought about what businesses rented the upstairs spaces.

As I watched Dana, still dressed in her stained-glass top, talking to someone out of sight, I dwelled on her lie about her where-abouts the morning of the murder. Sud-denly she turned to look out the window, and I plastered myself against the counter, hopefully out of her line of vision.

It seemed out of character for her to have

fishy two-hour gaps in her schedule. And now this. What was she doing upstairs in the murky precincts over Sprouts, especially when she hadn't mentioned it to me? She mentions *everything.*

Just as she turned away from the open window and I took the opportunity to leap out of the restaurant and dash over to the honeysuckle bushes, something incredible happened. Dana started to pull her colorful top over her head.

"You okay?" said Jimi Baker, coming back to the job, slipping his phone into his back pocket. I was speechless. I thought I knew Dana. She was so ultimately knowable, considering how much she talked and how uncomplicated she seemed. Do uncomplicated people have secrets? Maybe so. Maybe even more. Maybe they only seem uncomplicated because they've packed away all the things they want to keep from other people.

As I stood there, mute, Jimi patted me absently on the shoulder and got back to work. I slunk along the stockade fence until I was out of sight of that third-floor window, just in case the shade flew back open. When I reached the sidewalk, I realized my heart was pounding because I was spying on a friend. I turned right, toward Sprouts, forcing a smile at the wandering Akahana, who headed slowly toward me in her serpentine way, frowning.

And just past Sprouts, there was a black door in a small alcove that led up to the offices on the upper floors of the Logan Building. A directory listed the tenants. On the third floor was a dentist, a psychic, a photographer, a massage therapist named Henrik Blom, and the offices of Veganopoly, Inc., the parent company of Sprouts.

Well, unless the dentist's definition of filling cavities had nothing to do with teeth, I could eliminate him. And unless the psychic told fortunes by reading something other than palms, I could eliminate her. And since Veganopoly was probably not in a position to promote Dana, I couldn't see how they'd interest her in the least.

So either Dana was having sexy shots taken for the smitten Patrick, or coordinating Operation Free Maria Pia had given her a backache that required attention.

I let myself into the building and padded quickly up the marble stairs to the second floor, where I made the turn and — heart pounding — flowed up to the third floor. What if she suddenly came out into the hallway? What was my cover? I darted around the west side of the hall and discovered the offices of Veganopoly and the dentist. That left the psychic, the masseur, and the photographer on the east side of the hallway, closest to Miracolo. Dana was in there somewhere, half dressed behind a drawn shade.

Well, she wouldn't believe me if I told her I was getting my fortune told. Besides, the sign said Closed.

She knew I already had a dentist down in Philly.

Photos? Massage? Something to do with Sprouts?

Yes, that was it. Just a casual, spur-of-the-moment drop-by at Veganopoly to see whether Sprouts was going to do anything during the annual Market Square sidewalk sale. That was plausible.

But Dana didn't come out, and pressing my ear to the door didn't yield a thing.

Until, that is, the door to Massage Mania suddenly opened, and what I can only assume was the beefy Henrik escorted an old bald guy out of the office. I looked at my watch as though I was waiting for someone, and then looked again while Henrik explained to the departing client that a bath with Epsom salts would now rid him of toxins. They headed for the stairs.

So that left the photographer at the end of the hall. Pixie's Pix. And this had to be the place with the window facing Miracolo's courtyard. The sign on the door touted graduation, wedding, and commercial photography and gave their hours. A big yellow starburst sticker screamed a half-price special on "glamour shots."

Since Dana was past the wedding, way past the graduation, and had no commerce that required commercial shots, I decided that she was in there taking advantage of the half-price special. Aside from the fact that glamour shots were weird, and weird often appealed to her, what could she possibly have in mind? And did it have anything to do with what she was really doing the morning of Arlen Mather's murder?

And what kind of glamour shots are topless? Or better yet, naked?

Was Pixie Pix a front for something . . . *else*?

I discovered I could hang out in the kiddy playground in the center of Providence Park and keep an eye on the black door leading to the upstairs offices in the Logan Building. The benches were still wet from the rain, so I skulked, half hidden by the yellow-and-orange climbing gym. Fortunately, there were enough moms sipping lattes and yakking it up while their kids pleaded for a push on the wet swings or help coming down the rain-slick slide that I blended in pretty well.

At 3:20 p.m., subject Dana Cahill was seen leaving the Logan Building. Fully dressed.

I stayed in the park a while longer, while she made her way down the street, then I crossed the north side of Market Square and let myself back into Miracolo. Jimi Baker had done a nice job on the new lock. And now there were only two keys — and I had both of them. Life was better than good.

I was halfway across the dining room, where I could never get enough of the cathedral-like silence and cool air, when there was a quick, hard knock at the front door. In walked Joe Beck and Ted the detective. Joe shot me a brief "Hey," and the three of us stood around in the peaceful semidarkness for a few seconds while our eyes adjusted.

Joe was wearing a French-blue shirt under a light leather jacket spattered with raindrops, what could only be called pussycat-gray pants, and low boots. Patrick Cahill looks like he teaches American history at Exeter; Joe Beck looks like he *is* American history. "How've you been?" he asked me.

It struck me I hadn't seen him around for a day. Maybe he was chasing Kayla through the kale out at the farm. "Fine, fine, getting back to normal. You?"

"Working." He leaned against the piano that would soon become acquainted with the glorious Mrs. Crawford.

Then I raised my eyebrows at Ted. "What brings you to our fair restaurant?" I crossed my arms, waiting to be grilled about my grandmother or Dana. I kept my face blank, silently coaching myself to give nothing away.

Once the two men left, I'd try to reason my way through the events of the last couple of days. The little voice inside that sours everyone's dreams was whispering snidely, *You're a dancer, not a reasoner.*

Ted explained, "The forensics report came back a little while ago."

"And?" Boy, this heart of mine sold me out every time, picking up the beat even while I pretended indifference.

Joe pushed himself away from the Yamaha. "Your grandmother's boyfriend died of blunt force trauma, so no news there."

"Right." I looked back and forth between the two men. What were they getting around to? And when? One of them was wearing an

Hermès men's cologne I recognized from the perfume aisle, where it always made me stop dead in my tracks. It was like hypnosis in a spray bottle. Could it be Ted? If so, I needed to learn his last name.

"Coroner's putting the time of death around ten a.m.," said Ted, who swaggered close enough that the smell of garlic and onions took him right out of the running as the Hermès wearer. "Could go as early as nine thirty, but no later than eleven."

And Dana hadn't shown up at Cahill Enterprises until 11:30.

There had to be an explanation. One that didn't include murder. Or sexy time at Pixie Pix.

"Your grandmother can't account for her movements during the critical time," the detective continued.

How did he know that? According to Landon, she'd told the cops she dropped Arlen off and went on her way. Had Landon missed the alibi part? Had Maria Pia?

Joe was looking at me a little too earnestly.

I crossed my arms to steady myself. "Well, what did she say?" I asked Ted.

"She *said* she dropped him off sometime after nine and headed for Philly. Something about a dress."

I shrugged. "I guess she went shopping."

"Eve," said Joe, "she'll need to name some folks who can corroborate her story. Otherwise —"

"— it's not looking good," Detective Ted finished.

The world was suddenly a place where the choice was between saving a lying, deceitful friend or a lying, deceitful, and annoying grandmother. At the end of the day, crazy blood was thicker than crazy water. But I wanted to protect them both. After Joe and Ted left, I poured myself a grappa, which is great if what you want in a drink is nail polish remover that won't kill you. Then I slumped over the bar.

Where was Maria Pia tooling around on the morning of the murder? How big and bad could it be? So bad that she couldn't come clean with Landon, Choo Choo, and me? Not to mention the cops? The more I thought about it, the more nervous I got. My poor mind kept going into those dark corners where nothing lives except fierce-eyed madness, giggling at you in the dark.

What if Maria Pia had joined forces with Belladonna Russo and they were up to major culinary no good?

What if she was opening up a branch location of Miracolo and freezing us all out?

What if she was cheating on poor Arlen, who, to hear her tell it, was practically my stepgrandfather?

The best antidote for raging paranoia was time spent with Choo Choo. Back in college, I came across the word *phlegmatic* in a medieval literature class, where I learned two important things. One was that *phlegmatic* meant someone unexcitable and not quick to display emotion, which right away made me think of my big cousin, and the other was that I could pretty much catch up on my sleep in the back row of the lecture hall.

Choo Choo (Giuseppe) Bacigalupo was the son of Maria Pia's only daughter, Serena, who married into the Brooklyn Bacigalupo family of rich undertakers. Into this crowd of Bacigalupos, who were surprisingly fun, were born Choo Choo and his younger sister, Little Serena.

Little Serena, who was 5 feet 11 and 220 pounds, had left for Disney World — "I want to live the magic!" — right after high school and had worked her way up to running the Buzz Lightyear Space Ranger ride. Due to this thinking outside the Italian bread box, Maria Pia never mentioned her. All the rest of us got tired of correcting her whenever she said of me, "My only granddaughter!"

So, with my muddle over the mysterious misdeeds of Maria Pia Angelotta, I felt greatly relieved when the door to Miracolo swung open, followed by the towering presence of my cousin, dressed in khakis and a roomy black shirt.

"Bella," he greeted me.

I jumped off my stool for a Choo Choo hug, the kind that aligns your spine, stimulates your liver, and makes you thankful he likes you. His head had been shaved and oiled and it was topped with a pair of Ray-Bans.

I touched the diamond stud in his ear. "Very nice," I told him, "very nice indeed." I looked him over while his pretty hazel eyes narrowed at me expectantly. I stroked my chin. "I think the look is 'Mr. Clean meets Tony Soprano' and then they jam together."

"Too Mr. Clean?"

I spread my hands. "It's you, Chooch."

He chewed his lip. "Too jazz musician?"

"Have you seen our new piano player, Mrs. Crawford? I think she sets the bar."

"Haven't met her."

"We're reopening tomorrow for dinner. You'll meet her then."

"Who's working?"

"Paulette and Vera." Though God knew

136

what kind of crowd we'd get after a homicide. I stepped behind the bar. "Get you something? A Coke?" His usual drink of choice, which he bought by the case from Sam's Club.

Choo Choo lifted a mitt. "Nothing for me." Then he went on: "You should bring in Alma and take Jonathan off wine, put him on tables. We're going to need him."

I leaned across the bar. "What are you talking about? After a murder, we'll be lucky if even the regulars come back." I never thought I'd pine for "Three Coins in the Fountain," but there you are.

Choo Choo's smile pushed his eyes into little crescents. It was the look I usually got from him and Landon when they thought I was being naïve. Needless to say, I got the look a lot. It's not so much that I'm naïve, it's that the two of them busy themselves in gossip of all sorts and take it for unimpeachable truth.

If I didn't believe Brad and Angelina were in trouble, I got the look. If I didn't believe that was a baby bump on Kim Kardashian, I was being naïve. But they didn't have a clue about anything truly useful, like local gossip — if they did, maybe they could explain to me what our songbird Dana was doing removing her top on the third floor of the Logan Building. I decided to keep this puzzling little bit of misbehavior to myself for a while.

Choo Choo pulled a rolled-up magazine out of his back pocket and set it between us on the bar. "Eve, murder is good for business."

"Bah!" I flipped a hand at him in a very Maria Pia kind of way.

Choo Choo gave me a knowing little smile. "Trust your Choo Choo, *bella;* tomorrow night you'll be thinking we're a truck stop outside Nashville. Too bad Mr. Mather didn't meet his maker here in the dining room. The gawkers are really going to get in your way."

Was he right? I sagged. Were there going to be all sorts of customer ruses to get into my kitchen — to praise the veal, condemn the risotto, equivocate about the snails — in order to eye the Spot? Maybe we should just point to some place close to the piano, I thought, looking around like a wild woman. Mrs. Crawford could handle anything.

"No!" I told Choo Choo. "I refuse!" I declared. "Miracolo will not capitalize on what happened to that poor unfortunate."

Choo Choo lightly tapped the magazine, then pushed it toward me. I picked up the old issue of *Inside Bucks County,* the local What to Do, Where to Eat, Whom to Envy rag. "Page twenty-three," he said phlegmatically.

The page turned out to be "County Doings," the lowdown on fancy parties. And there it was. One of the photos showed the glitterati who attended the Roller Ball, a gala two years ago that raised money for kids with spinal cord injuries. And there was Dana Mahoney Cahill, laughing it up with a martini glass in her hand. On one side of her was Patrick, looking quietly classy in a tux. But on the other side . . .

On the other side of Dana, the guy she had her arm around, was our very own gawker magnet: Arlen Mather. Only that wasn't the name in the caption. Under the photo was the caption *L to R: Patrick Cahill, Dana Cahill, and Maximiliano Scotti.*

8

I lay sleepless in bed, tangled in the ratty quilt I had had since I was two, trying to figure out what it all meant. Choo Choo had said the dude in the photo sure looked like Nonna's dead boyfriend, hey? Whereupon I had to grill him: "How do you know what Mather looked like?" He wasn't around when Landon and I discovered the body.

Then Chooch told me he'd been in the company of Arlen and Maria Pia about half a dozen times.

To which I responded, "Are you freaking kidding me?"

Apparently our nonna (though, as I lay there, I was willing to sign over my nonna rights to him and Landon forever, eternally and in perpetuity) had included Choo Choo when she and the beau went to Lancaster County for the day, Atlantic City for the night, and Manhattan for Chinese food. I was surprised by the strength of my jealousy. Yes, he has his appeal, but . . .

Not even a second grappa helped.

So the Volvo and I wended our way home to the tiny house I called home for the last three years. On the edge of the Quaker Hills Historic District was a piece of property owned by an old Philly choreographer who still, at eighty-four, dreamed of building on the site. She rented a corner of it to me, and I'd bought a Tumbleweed Tiny Home for $50,000 and had it delivered on a utility trailer to this little spot.

My house was a whopping 130 square feet of wonderfulness, with cedar siding and a tin roof that always made me long for rain. I set out big pots of splashy red geraniums and kept a little blue folding butterfly chair out front on my four-by four-foot porch, where I hung a wind chime.

The tiny home had everything I required: a sleeping loft; a two-burner stove, since I saved all my serious cooking for the restaurant; and lots of windows due to my love of light and air. I guess I'm no different from the geraniums out front.

I looked at the stars out the window in my sleeping loft, telling myself that if Nonna had something up her sleeve, she'd use Choo Choo to help her keep it there. If

Dana had been fraternizing with a dead guy with two different names, it probably just had something to do with a pompous stage name (Maximiliano Scotti? Really?) and not a double identity.

All of which goes to show that if you really want to fool yourself, you have to go big.

I was wrong about all of it.

Thursday

The next day, Miracolo became like a Disney cartoon where mice or candlesticks are furiously furnishing a banquet, bearing impossible things on their heads, and singing their little animated hearts out. All of our suppliers showed up at once — the linens, the uniforms, the wholesalers. I actually wrung my hands when I stood at our propped-open front door and heard the griping car horns trying to get around the fleet of double-parked delivery trucks.

Paulette showed up early to play quartermaster and direct the action, freeing me up to figure out the specials. To keep the mayhem to a minimum, I decided to go with two easy but elegant vegetable pasta dishes, *pansotti* and *piccage,* and call it Vegetarian Night. As I wrote them up on the specials board, I could already hear Maria Pia's complaints. But I was hoping she was so distracted by Arlen/Maximiliano's murder that she would just let me be.

At 2:53 p.m., Choo Choo and Paulette were laying out the table linens.

Landon — who found a backup mortar and pestle — was making pesto for my *piccage* and happily discussing the career of Liza Minnelli with Jonathan.

Alma and Vera were filling vases. Alma was pouring the water and Vera was standing nearby with towels to mop up the spillage. She shot me a long-suffering look, a cross between *What's with her?* and *Patience, someday we'll be all be clumsy dinosaurs, too.*

Kayla, dressed in layers of pastel gauze, was singing a Nora Jones medley and setting out greens and potatoes on the counter.

And then the double doors to the kitchen slammed open. "So now we're asking the altar boys to perform the Mass?"

Jonathan stepped closer to Landon, who didn't mind in the least.

I turned, brushing whole wheat flour from my hands. "What are you talking about, Nonna?" said I innocently.

"*Vegetarian* Night at Miracolo? Really, Eve?" Maria Pia was wearing a Saks version of widow's weeds, a black drop-waist, high-collar dress.

"Yes, and it's going to be great."

Her nostrils flared at me. "You know how I feel about vegetables."

You'd think she was accusing me of selling state secrets and shoving compromising photos under my nose.

So I recited the Maria Pia catechism. "Fine in their place, but handmaidens to the beef and fish and chicken."

"Exactly," she tipped her head in semiapproval. "So it's not too late —"

But it was. And as much as I loved her, it wasn't fine to be that unbending on somebody else's watch. "Nonna, if your boyfriend hadn't gotten himself killed here, maybe I would have had time to do something more ambitious."

She gasped. Outside the double doors I could see Paulette, Alma, Vera, and Choo Choo crammed together, watching. "That's a terrible —"

I plowed on. "But he did, so guess what? Today the altar boys are performing the Mass."

It was a standoff, the two of us staring each other down, our arms crossed. Then she suddenly sank into a fine old mope. "Well, at least it isn't . . . cannoli." She could hardly form the hated word.

With that, Choo Choo and the others slid aside and let her back into the dining room.

When she was gone, complaining loudly about greens and calling me her least favorite granddaughter — brava, Little Serena, you're suddenly back in the mix — I sank against the prep table, fanning myself with my chef's hat.

Landon dashed over to me and wrapped me in a hug. "You prevailed," he said, eyes filled with wonder.

"Believe me," I said to him, "I'll pay for it."

He waved it away. "She'll forget all about it." I think he was just basking in the afterglow of shielding Jonathan from the Dragon of Market Square.

When the noise level rose out in the dining room, I peeked through the round windows. Mrs. Crawford had arrived, resplendent in a black-and-teal cocktail dress, black fishnet stockings and snood over her wiry brown hair, the predictable matching heels, and elbow-length gloves. Ready for work.

For my grandmother, coming face-to-face with Mrs. Bryce Crawford was like spying a sooty likeness of the Blessed Mother on the broad side of a barn. She was speechless. In her, speechlessness can go either way: either she's winding up to a tirade, or the cause of her wordlessness achieves some strange iconic status in her weird psyche.

I was betting that Mrs. Crawford was going to be the human equivalent of the dreaded cannoli.

Landon elbowed me in the ribs.

Unaware, Vera and Choo Choo kept setting tables. Alma was now refilling the salt and pepper shakers, and Paulette was rearranging the mat in the foyer.

Mrs. Crawford and Maria Pia each extended a queenly hand to the other, waiting for some serfish slavering that was not forthcoming, so just a light shake ensued. When my grandmother turned away from our newest hire, I saw that I'd been wrong. No tirade was coming. She actually looked kind of cowed, muttering something that sounded like *buona fortuna* to our pianist as she headed for the bar, where ordinarily she never goes.

At the sound of a rap on the glass of our back door, I turned to see Joe Beck step inside.

"Hey," said Kayla.

"Hey," said Joe. He took a deep breath that I'd like to think had nothing to do with the nearness of my second cousin, and motioned me over.

Everyone else followed, and I found myself standing in a tight little knot in the middle

146

of the kitchen floor, not far from where Arlen had fallen.

He gave the others a quick glance and then looked at me. "Where's your grandmother?" he asked in a low voice.

"Out front." I eyed him closely. "Why? Do you want me to call her in?"

Joe shook his head. "I just want to give you a heads-up. The cops have found a witness."

We all looked at each other like it was good news.

"So someone came forward?" breathed Landon.

For some reason, Joe did not look happy. He gave a little nod. "A DIRECTV installer."

"Okay . . ." I said slowly, wondering where this was going. Did the guy see Dana follow Mather into the restaurant to take care of a little business before reporting to work at Cahill Enterprises? Poor Dana. Poor Patrick.

Joe rammed his hands into his pocket. "He was on the block the morning of the murder."

"And?" prompted Paulette.

"They showed him some pictures of key people, and the guy made a positive ID."

"Dana?" I breathed.

"Choo Choo?" whispered Landon, knobbing a fist at his mouth.

"Landon?" Kayla guessed. At which we all turned to her.

Joe looked like he couldn't see any way around it. Finally he said, "He's prepared to testify that he saw Maria Pia enter the restaurant at ten thirty a.m."

My heart was pounding. From the dining room came the sounds of Mrs. Crawford at the piano, accompanying Nonna in her lusty cover of Judy Collins's "Both Sides Now." She was up to the line that went, *Bows and floes of angel hair, and ice cream castles in the air, and feathered canyons everywhere . . .* "And the coroner puts the time of death at . . ." I struggled to recall what I'd heard.

"Between nine thirty and eleven thirty," said Joe, looking grim.

Tears stung my eyes.

When Joe touched my shoulder, I actually sobbed. Landon wasn't far behind. "Sally and Ted are on their way over. The fingerprints on the murder weapon came back a match for your grandmother."

My heart battered against my chest. "She uses the mortar!" I cried.

He raised an eyebrow at me. "That's what they're saying."

"For grinding," I went on, my voice a little

high, and I swiped a dish towel at him. "Like I do."

He shook his head. "Sorry, Eve, just hers. I came because I thought you could prepare her for —"

Suddenly the music stopped.

We opened the doors to the dining room, where we saw Ted, Sally, and a uniformed police woman. Mrs. Crawford's fingers floated above the piano keys, and Choo Choo held a napkin aloft.

Nonna gaily chided the newcomers, shooing them away in full grande dame mode. "I'm so sorry, but we don't open until five p.m. If you want to return then for Vegetarian Night, we can —"

Ted grimly said, "Maria Pia Angelotta —"

"Yes?" she said, waiting for him to get on with it. Which, considering her supreme self-confidence, she probably thought was going to be some civic award.

Poor Ted looked like he'd rather be off somewhere fishing in the rain. "I'm placing you under arrest for the murder of Arlen Mather."

"No!" shouted Landon, who flung himself into my arms, and we gripped each other like our lives depended on it.

Nonna looked at Detective Ted as if she

couldn't quite comprehend what he was saying.

His hands stuffed in his pockets, Ted rolled on, "You have the right to remain silent. Anything you say or do can and will be held against you —"

If you can pass out without falling down, I think that's what I did.

9

How we all got through the next eight hours, I'll never know. I made the *pansotti* and *piccage,* but I could have been fashioning little people out of Play-Doh for all it mattered to me. At the moment of the arrest, Choo Choo declared he would follow Nonna down to the Bucks County jail. In his absence, he deputized Paulette to seat people. The woman who could kill fish with her bare hands actually seemed choked up at the responsibility.

Even in her shock, Maria Pia insisted we go ahead with the reopening. We all kissed her repeatedly and promised a lawyer, a kimono, and a copy of *Gourmet.*

For me she had a special message, clasping my shoulders, and giving me her Obi-Wan Kenobi look: "Remember, Eve, food is the art" — she paused for effect — "we eat."

Huh? I murmured, "Yes, Nonna, I'll remember." I let out a little sob.

Then off she went, a tragic figure wrapped in a silver shawl, snagging a handful of after dinner mints from the dish by the door, fol lowed by Quaker Hills's finest.

And Choo Choo.

Who, by the way, had accurately predicted the evening's trade.

Halfway into the mêlée of that night, Gian carlo recruited his twentysomething bike grandson to help behind the bar. Nobody even noticed the chains and Grateful Dead T-shirt.

Our Lady of Reduced Circumstances Alma, managed to break two water glasses and one antipasto plate. Had the woman always been this clumsy? I didn't think so she was just unnerved by the murder.

Even so, she found many opportunities to model the shoes on her feet, fabric painted to depict the nursery rhyme about the old woman who lived in a shoe. All the chil dren's heads were beads. Landon whispered to me that for a woman who had the fin motor skills to apply tiny crap to shoes, she sure broke a lot of stuff.

Paulette was everywhere all at once, truly the evening's field marshal.

Dana, when she waltzed in wearing a midnight-blue sheath, fretted about Maria Pia's arrest because now who was going to harmonize with her on "Those Were the Days"? She also argued with Paulette, who wanted her to bring out the bread and fill water glasses; Dana claimed it might confuse the customers, seeing the chanteuse perform a menial task.

Paulette pointed out that there's nothing the little people like more than seeing a celebrity act like a real person, but no dice.

Mrs. Crawford kept customers without reservations happy with a patter I suspected was a little bawdier than Maria Pia would have condoned. Sadly, I couldn't get close enough to tell.

Li Wei's, hair stuck up farther as the evening wore on and the tower of dirty dishes mounted.

Kayla amazingly stuck around, washing, slicing, chopping, and peeling vegetables. She managed to stay normal for a full eight hours.

The first time I looked up from the three different sauces simmering on my beloved Vulcan, I saw Joe Beck toothpicking rolled prosciutto onto sliced melon. The second time I looked up, Landon was giving him a crash course in the Art of the Garnish.

Eye Candy Jonathan seemed to sharpen up under the general stress. He slipped in his wine knowledge wherever appropriate, and acted like he'd been waiting tables since his toddler days.

Landon worked at triple his usual speed, and still found time to talk about how cute Jonathan was.

From my place in the kitchen, I could barely hear the piano over the clinking glasses and boisterous chatter. Nonna would have loved it. A few customers pretended to get lost on the way to the bathroom, detouring into the murder kitchen until Paulette headed them off. Many others just pumped the staff for the exquisite details, which were further embellished with every telling.

When the crowd thinned out around 10 p.m., the regulars started tuning up. Mrs. Crawford eyed them kind of speculatively while she adjusted her black fishnet snood.

We kitchen troglodytes finally spilled out into the dining room and slipped into seats at the table in the farthest corner. Landon draped himself on me, while Joe held on to a Corona and Kayla made out a bill for services rendered.

I was too tired even to care, but it was gratifying to see Joe shoot her a disbelieving look. I caught his eye.

Meanwhile, Dana worked the room that now consisted of just our homegrown amateur musicians and bartender Giancarlo

Crespi, uttering some witty repartee into her microphone. For a friend who seemed generally as complex as instant chocolate pudding — and I really like chocolate pudding — apparently she was managing Olympic-level deceit in her off-hours. It was still amazing to me. What explained it?

As the talk at our table turned to the murder, nobody had much of an answer when soft-spoken Alma asked who we thought could have done it. "Some maniac," muttered Kayla, and I only hoped it was some maniac we didn't know. Over the course of the evening, Alma's nursery-rhyme Toscano's Tootsies had shed some children's heads, and even the fake feathers looked wilted. She sat with her tired legs splayed, one hand shaking as it rested on the table.

It had been a very long night, and at the point when our chins were sinking closer to the table, Paulette took one look at us, disappeared into the kitchen, and brought out the leftover tiramisu.

As she cut slices, Dana started warbling "The Shadow of Your Smile," leaning provocatively over Roy, the regular who played the bongos. Suddenly Mrs. Crawford was weighing in with some experimental chords in accompaniment. The mandolin, the guitars, the homemade bass, the bongos, and the clarinet pulled back in awe as Dana got in touch with her inner diva and swanned around the dining room, beaming at me for finally providing her with a proper accompanist.

Mrs. Crawford moved into a jazz riff, leaving Dana to play catch-up. As Alma waved us all good night and dragged herself out the front door, Giancarlo brought over the bar receipts. Suddenly Vera erupted into a gorgeous scat on "The Shadow of Your Smile" that fit beautifully with Mrs. Crawford's playful improv.

Paulette gave an appreciative whistle, the kind that summons New York cabs in a downpour, and disappeared into the kitchen with a stack of plates. Landon actually pulled me out of my chair, moving to the beat in a bossa nova step. Since I'd been on my feet for the last eight hours, I could hardly feel my legs, but I joined him, laughing.

Still in our chef jackets, we clasped hands and oozed through the box step, the two-step, and the chassé. When the song ended, Jonathan clapped wildly, and Joe lifted his bottle at me with a grin.

Dana's smile was strained, but then she slid off into her signature song: "For you,

Maria Pia, wherever you are!" — had no one told her? — "Three Coins in the Fountain." Whereupon Mrs. Crawford reached for her elbow-length gloves and the others got up to clear our table. Kayla and I were left sitting there and she put her feet up on an empty chair, her gauzy layers falling in every direction.

I noticed her beige ballet flats, decorated with glitter in the shape of a slug's trail. "Alma's shoes?" I asked her, gesturing toward her feet.

"Yeah," said Kayla, pushing her bill across the table to me. I just folded it in half. "Oh, wait," she added, pulling a little Peruvian-print shoulder bag over her head and digging around in it. She came up with a stack of business cards held together with a tiny red plastic banana clip. "I know Alma is crap as far as waitressing goes, but she's a brilliant designer."

The cheap clip broke apart, and cards cascaded off the table. Kayla swore, topping even Dana, who had gotten to "Make it mine! Make it mine! Make it mine!" I leaned over to help pick them up, while Kayla, for some harebrained reason, decided to give me the romantic details of her couch time with Joe Beck. Before she got very far, I screamed, "Encore!" at Dana, who needed no further encouragement.

As I raked up fallen business cards, I saw that my kiss-and-tell cousin went to a chiropractor, a tanning place, an acupuncturist, a Rolfer, and something called a polarity therapist. How she afforded these services growing onions and kale was a mystery. She had cards for the Penn State Agricultural Extension Agency, The Warped Sisters' Weavers' Cooperative, Greyhound Adoption, Yurts of America . . . and Arlen Mather.

Burgundy lettering on buff card stock read Arlen Mather, ASID, with a couple of contact numbers. Already more information on the murdered man than I had. And until I figured where to take the Calladine's Classics line of inquiry, I might have a new direction. I pushed the other cards back to Kayla, then waved Arlen's at her. "What's this?" I asked.

She leaned toward me, squinting. Then she very helpfully said, "That's Arlen's business card."

"I can see that. Why do you have it?"

Kayla got all shruggy on me, which was her "tell." "You know how you just pick things up," she said evasively. I stared at her, waiting. "Here and there."

I studied the card, then looked over at her.

"Did you hire him?"

She stared at me, wide-eyed. "Hire him?" Then she brayed like it was just too funny. To break the tension, I turned to look at the musicians. Dana launched into her version of "You're So Vain," which always seemed to miss the point of the lyrics and sounded more like a wow-my-boyfriend's-so-cool kind of song.

"Yeah," I turned back to Kayla, "did you hire him?" Having absolutely no idea what ASID stood for, I fudged it. "I mean, he was a member of ASID, so —"

She circled an arm at me diagonally in that gesture that translates as *perhaps purée-ing your brain with some garlic and basil would improve it.* "Why would I need an interior designer, Eve? I live on a frickin' farm."

"You have a house."

She shot me a look like I had been released prematurely from a psych ward. "I have a yurt."

How long had it been since I'd driven out to Kale & Kayla Organics?

Singing, Dana gushed, " 'You had one eye in the mirror as you watched yourself gavotte.' " Then she did her interpretation of the gavotte, which bore a strong resemblance to Michael Jackson's moonwalk.

Maybe I could get her to work up "Billie Jean."

"Okay," I said, "so if you didn't use his design services, why do you have his business card?" I tried to make it sound like I hadn't just asked that same question.

"None of your sweet business, cuz," she said with an unpleasant smile.

"None of my *business*?" I slammed a hand on the table. "This," I said in my best *Law & Order* voice, "is a murder investigation. Arlen Mather was bludgeoned to death in our kitchen, which is why we all just worked our asses off tonight, and why I just received a bill from you." I slapped the offending bill with the back of my hand. "Because I guess *you* don't see this as a family matter." Maria Pia couldn't have done it better. She didn't do guilt trips; she did guilt safaris.

Kayla sulked. "Oh, all right, forget the bill."

I took a deep breath and circled back, saying slowly, like I was translating for her, "Why do you have Arlen Mather's —"

"He gave it to me, if you must know!" she shouted.

"No kidding." Did she think that was some kind of answer? "When?"

"None of your —"

I overrode her. *"When!"*

"The first time we slept together," she flung at me.

First. Time. Slept. Together.

I think I had a stroke. I couldn't make those words work together in any meaningful way. Not when I arranged them anywhere near Arlen and Mather. I shuffled them around. Together, Mather, time, Arlen, slept, first. The fact that it actually helped worried me all the more that I'd had a stroke.

While I stammered, Kayla rolled her eyes, saying something like *hopeless prude.* I think it was the image that was doing me in. I was still having a hard time not picturing her with Joe. But picturing her with Arlen Mather was like learning that pasta has feelings or crop circles are the work of leprechauns.

So Kayla was the woman Mather had broken up with for my nearly octogenarian grandmother. I guess he was an equal opportunity scum bucket. Although there may have been an element of self-preservation there. Maria Pia just needed to be dealt with. Kayla needed to be strategized, the way a mongoose dances around a cobra.

All I could manage, finally, was: "Does

Nonna know?"

She made a noise that sounded like "Chuh."

"No, really, Kayla," I said with some heat. "Does she?"

Sighing extravagantly, she pulled her hair up into one of the blue rubber bands she uses to band together heads of broccoli. "Who knows *what* that woman knows, Eve. You know what I'm talking about?" Our eyes locked in understanding. "I sure didn't tell her."

Did I detect some intrigue? Did my cousin fear blowback from my nonna, who might take a dim view of sharing her deceased beloved with a rival forty years younger? It was just the sort of goofy position Maria Pia might take.

I was struck by a thought. "Did you and Arlen go to an opera fund-raiser together about eight months ago?"

"Yeah, why?"

So she must have been the "daughter" in pearls and a feathered boa described by Mrs. Crawford. Back then, Kayla's hair was platinum blond and ironed straight.

At that point, Dana was belting out *Well, I hear you went up to Saratoga, and your horse naturally won,* holding the poor microphone with one hand while the other was whipping her own flank. It looked vaguely suggestive and the music-making regulars were whooping. One of these days we'd have to have a heart-to-heart. . . .

There were other ways of looking at Kayla's keeping her Arlen affair a secret. For one, maybe she was lying. One week she'll tell me airily that she hadn't planted any escarole, and then the next week she'd show up with bushels of the stuff. Kayla always worked from a deep and abiding belief in her own convenience.

So maybe she didn't tell Maria Pia directly about Arlen Mather, but made sure it got back to her. A well-placed hint here or there to a couple of gabby Miracolo customers would do the trick.

Or maybe Kayla wanted to spare Maria Pia any pain or embarrassment.

No, that probably wouldn't even make it into the top ten of possible motives.

"So you didn't tell her you were the former girlfriend?"

"Are you kidding me?" Kayla actually squeaked. "Auntie Maria Pia's such a wild card" — an example of the pot calling the kettle cookware — "I didn't want to take a chance on her freezing me out of the local restaurant trade."

I was unconvinced. Grow a good eggplant,

and Maria Pia Angelotta was yours for life. She'd never let personal feelings interfere with her culinary destiny. Surely Kayla knew that.

There was something my dear cousin Kayla wasn't telling me. But what? I wasn't thinking diabolically enough. *Think like Kayla.*

And then it hit me.

Kayla hadn't told Maria Pia that she was Arlen Mather's former girlfriend because . . . she wasn't *former.* Maybe his business card wasn't the only thing Arlen Mather was giving Kayla on the side. She'd like the intrigue. She'd like the joke.

Then, what if Maria Pia found out and . . . took a blunt object to her two-timing beau?

The room suddenly got colder.

There was no way I would telegraph that suspicion to the cobra sitting across from me. Nonna was already facing prison food. I wouldn't be responsible for prolonging that experience.

Kayla was giving me what Landon and I call her "lock-down look." Eyes wide open so she looks all gee-whiz frank, but the battle-scarred among us know there's a force field she slides over her corneas to keep you from penetrating her secrets. Oh, she'll give them up (and yours) on a mere whim, but she'll do anything she can to keep you from guessing them on your own.

And then an even more chilling thought struck me.

As bad as the possibility of Kayla's carrying on with Nonna's boyfriend behind her back was, there was yet another explanation for Arlen Mather's murder. What if my self-indulgent cousin hadn't liked being dumped by her elderly boyfriend? Did being kicked to the curb make her mad? Mad enough for murder?

If so, I was tempted to get her the worst lawyer money could buy.

Finally, I was able to smile.

10

"Night," said Joe, one of the last to leave. When all the cleanup was done, he had rolled down his sleeves and argued with Paulette about a bottle of Barbaresco she had tried to press on him by way of saying thanks for the help. Paulette won. When he gave her a kiss on the cheek, she fluttered a work-roughened hand at him and called him a silly man.

He held up the bottle and looked at me. "I'll save it for a special occasion," he said with a smile.

"When Nonna comes home?" I piped up.

"That would qualify," he said very seriously.

But I had the sudden feeling that wasn't what he'd meant.

Jonathan, Vera, Mrs. Crawford — I'd invited her for a drink the next day, part of my plot to lay the gender issue to rest — Giancarlo, Dana, Li Wei, and the regulars had all slipped out nearly an hour ago, letting in the rasp of spring peepers from the woods beyond Callowhill Street. The stars seemed unusually close when I closed the door behind Vera, who was wrapping herself in a blue-spangled shawl, and I had the crazy thought of leaving my car parked on Market Square and just walking home.

"Come back anytime," Paulette told him with a pat on the back. "Right, Eve?"

I looked at Joe, standing in the doorway to the courtyard, backlit by the tiki lights and the moon. And I smiled at him, the good-looking guy who made tea for destabilized neighbors, the guy who could now garnish plates with the best of them.

"Anytime at all. Just watch out for the compost, Beck," I teased. We exchanged smiles that seemed to say we were already better friends than I knew, and something flashed between us that felt very nice indeed.

Raising the bottle in a salute, he was off.

Landon closed up the front and when the dining room went dark, Paulette and I waited for him by the back door. When he came into view in the semidarkness, we all smiled wanly and went out into the night. With as much satisfaction as I could muster at 12:47 a.m., I locked our brand-new

Schlage and followed them down the brick walk to the street.

On Market Square, the streetlights showed a deserted street. Though Jolly's Pub was still open, no one was spilling out the front door, either on their own or assisted by the frightening Adrian. Paulette called a final "good night!" and set off toward the parking garage two blocks away. I could feel Landon relax when we were finally alone, and we set off arm in arm toward our cars.

As we neared mine, I saw a towering figure lounging against the hood. Choo Choo.

We ran the rest of the way, flinging ourselves at Chooch, who wrapped his arms around both of us at once. Nobody cried; we were too tired.

"How's Nonna?" breathed Landon. His voice dropped. "Is she on . . . suicide watch?"

Choo Choo smoothed a beefy hand over his skull. "Nonna?" he asked, incredulous.

I knew what he meant: she puts *other* people on suicide watch.

"Is it awful?" I breathed. Knowing Maria Pia, instead of sweetening the jailer with smokes or chocolates, she'd antagonize him with hurled, untranslatable words and a hand gesture that pretty much tells him his ass looks like a turkey's tail feathers.

168

He shook his head. "When I left she was just sitting there on her bunk."

Landon looked earnest. "Upper or lower?" Somehow the answer mattered.

"Lower. No roommate. Yet."

This was a lot of information, so the three of us went silent for a minute.

Then Landon tried to sound chipper. "Sounds okay — I mean, doesn't it, *bella*?" He turned to face me. He looked more than usually anxious, and I couldn't say why.

Choo Choo just looked at me. "Nonna wants to see you tomorrow sometime, Eve."

"I was planning on it."

"She says be sure not to forget, because . . ."

As it registered that he was biting his lip, I took a step back. "Tell me, Choo Choo."

He slammed his hand on the hood of my car. Then he looked at us with a ragged, haunted expression. "She had motive, means, and opportunity, Eve. And she said she has something to confess."

Friday

I lay in the dark in my loft, faceup and uncovered, until the clock said almost 3:30 a.m. Who was Arlen Mather? And why was he playing at being someone named Maximiliano Scotti? Had he just put it on for the opera fund-raiser? What had he been up to? And what did it have to do with opera memorabilia? I just couldn't get a fix on our murder victim.

Still, there was one new clue.

On a whim I dug around for my phone and hit a number on speed dial that I hadn't called in quite some time. I knew he'd still be up, that insomniac, splendiferous dancer pal of mine. He answered, wide awake. "Angelotta?" came his happy bellow.

"Tone!" I was absurdly happy to hear the voice of Tony Treadwell. We talked for half an hour, Tony filling me in on some recent auditions, good, bad, and most definitely ugly. We laughed a lot. Things were good with Lila, his live-in girlfriend, and they had bought a dachshund and named him Nijinsky. I filled him in on the murder and my jailed nonna, and how there wasn't anything much happening in my love life. (Tony always gets the truth.)

Then Tony asked about my leg and when I was coming back.

What a funny notion. "To the City?"

"To dance, you goof!"

I felt so touched. There was still someone who viewed my defection three years ago as mere recuperation. I sniffed a little and told him I had no plans beyond tomorrow's menu.

"Listen, Tone, I need some info. Do you still see Veronica Gale?"

Veronica was the over-the-top set designer for an Off-Broadway musical about the lost city of Atlantis that Tony had played the second lead in. I'd remembered that she had the same creds as Arlen Mather: ASID I had googled it earlier, and discovered it stood for the American Society of Interior Designers. Veronica Gale might be able to take me a step further.

"Sure. All the time."

I explained what I needed him to find out from Veronica, and I had to get him to promise to wait until morning. Laughing, he agreed, and then he said he'd send me audition information for the upcoming revival of *The Boys from Syracuse.* I actually agreed to meet for lunch at the Broadway Deli sometime in the next two weeks.

When we hung up, I felt deeply happy. No, it wasn't happiness exactly. It was a quiet certainty that I had reconnected with an important part of my life. Tony stood for dance, for my life before my days and nights consisted of cooking northern Italian dishes. Lying there beneath the cool ceiling fan, I saw dance in the fan, I felt dance in my pulse, I heard dance in the rasp of the peepers in the woods.

But fans slow to a stop, pulses settle down, and peepers go away.

My Broadway dance career was over.

Now my life was all about Quaker Hills, Miracolo, and most important, my family.

My mind kept stealing back to Choo Choo's words: *She has something to confess.*

The words fell in rhythm with the fan as it spun in its slow, dependable circles.

Something to confess. Something to confess. Something to confess.

What could Nonna possibly have to confess? I would never believe that she would commit murder, so what could it be? I decided it had to have something to do with cooking. Something about a recipe. Something shocking. And then I talked myself into believing the absolute worst: that it was she, not that *strega* Belladonna Russo, who used the Stella D'oro ladyfingers in the recipe for her contest tiramisu.

And with that, I finally fell asleep.

In the warm morning light, over a couple of espresso shots in my butterfly chair while the sun burned off the dew, I wish I could tell you things looked better.

They did not.

Sometimes we really do expect too much from coffee.

The neighbor's poodle wandered over for his usual stroking and patting; then he gave me a reproachful look that seemed to say *Get over yourself,* and trotted off, his tags jingling. The birds, singing on branches backlit by the sun, didn't get it, either.

Nonna was in jail. Dana was sneaking around topless. Landon hadn't been this anxious since Kurt had come out to his dad on *Glee.* And Kayla was Kayla.

Which, for me, was a source of bafflement greater than why the cops thought my nonna had beaned her boyfriend. So she hadn't picked up the alterations from Saks. So she was seen entering Miracolo at the key time. You call that suspicious?

Because I certainly do.

This was a job for shopping therapy.

So I checked in with my key people. Choo Choo agreed to make the trip to the Philly fish market for the *fritto misto di pesce* special for that evening, and Paulette would drive out to our supplier to pick up our order of microgreens for garnish. We tossed out ideas for the dessert special, but nothing seemed right. My call to Landon went straight to voice mail. All the more reason for some serious trying on of overpriced clothes at Airplane Hangers.

I told them I'd pack Nonna a little over-night bag. By 10 a.m., I had watered my geraniums and stocked the glove compart-ment in the Volvo with a couple of bags of my favorite pico de gallo chips — the gusta-tory equivalent of Zoloft — and driven over to Nonna's. The house seemed depressed without her. As I stowed the latest issue of *Gourmet* and Nonna's favorite Chanel Precision Sublimage Essential Regenerating Crème into a green leather bag the size of Delaware, my hand paused.

And I had the feeling the French peasants must have experienced the moment it oc-curred to them they could storm the Bastille.

That evening's dessert special was sud-denly crystal clear.

With Nonna away, the cannoli would play.

At Airplane Hangers, I bought a low-cut, light jersey sleeveless dress in the shade of red that makes my chestnut hair look in-spired. I also bought it in black, which makes the rest of me look inspired. On my way back to the car, I spotted Dana on the south side of Market Square. Although everyone in Miracolo had keys to the restau-rant and could have followed Arlen Mather inside, Dana was the only one actually acting like she was up to no good.

Something made me keep my trap shut and hang back, because I swear she was acting furtive. And not flamboyantly furtive, which is how she acts when she wants to be caught at something. No, she honestly looked like she didn't want to run into anybody she knew. Which went a long way toward explaining the nondescript jacket and what could only be described as a fishing hat with a striped band, with the brim turned down.

Her chin-length black hair was tucked uncharacteristically behind her ears. And she was wearing sensible shoes with laces. She was so determined not to draw attention to herself that she wasn't even wearing sunglasses. Instead, she wore black-rimmed actual eyeglasses on her face, and I had never seen Dana in glasses.

Why the get-up?

With her hands stuffed into the pockets of a shapeless jacket the color of earthworms, she turned to look in a shop window when Akahana strolled by. The fact that it was the dry cleaner's didn't seem to matter. When Quaker Hills's only bag lady was far enough up the street that she must have felt safe, Dana continued up the south side of Market

Square. Past the antiques store, the home décor shop, and Tattie's. I followed at a safe distance, puzzled by Dana, buoyed by the thought of the rebel cannoli, impoverished by the two new therapeutic dresses.

At Jolly's Pub her hand reached for the door, but she drew it back when she caught sight of something through the window. Dana appeared to sag, stumped. Then she turned the far corner, running lightly in the sensible shoes she must have picked up at a thrift shop. At that, I ran, too, reached the corner, and peered around just in time to catch her slipping around the back of the building. My heart was pounding, less from the exercise than the sheer suspense. At the back, I listened for a second, heard a door opening, and peeked around the final corner. Dana was ducking into the back of Reginald Jolly's pub.

I darted down the alley toward the closing door.

I'd like to say I Saw All, but I was All at Sea. Maybe Dana and Reginald were smuggling porn out of the country via Arlen Mather's interior design business . . . somehow . . . and when Mather wanted a larger cut, they eliminated him. Or . . . Dana was having an affair with Reginald Jolly, of all people, and when Mather figured it out and tried a spot of blackmail ("Pay up or the Patrick Cahill gravy train stops here!"), Dana lured him to the restaurant and eliminated him.

But wait. Reginald didn't seem to know who Dana, the one who tricked him out of the key I had given him, was. Ha! I thought in a very Mr. Moto moment; he was blowing smoke at me, making me think he didn't know Dana.

I caught the closing door at the last moment, gripping it with my fingertips, holding it open a sliver. My ear strained to hear either smuggler talk or lover talk — poor Patrick, Knight of the Tassel Loafers — or, better yet, killer talk.

But . . . nothing.

Easing my fingertips off the door, I walked quickly around to the front of the building, edging toward the window to peer over the half-curtains. At 11:27 a.m., I was expecting to see Dana, but she was nowhere in sight. Neither was Reginald.

Then I squinted hard at the lone figure sitting at the bar, and my mouth fell open. "What?"

There, slumped over a martini, was Landon.

I furiously texted him, unsure whether I should ask him to explain himself or rescue him from that possible den of iniquity. I settled for *Meet me outside ASAP.* I watched him look at his phone, leave a bill on the bar, call out something to someone invisible, and head toward the door with his small Gucci backpack.

I startled him by grabbing his arm and walking us both across the street to Providence Park. Dodging moms and strollers on the paths to the center of the park, I ascertained that Landon had not seen Dana at the bar, and that Jonathan had not rebuffed his advances because he hadn't in point of fact made any, since it was still too much too soon and the lad wasn't ready for *l'amour.*

All satisfactory answers to truly important issues.

So, by process of shrewd elimination, that left Nonna. I told Landon that I'd packed her a bag that included things Choo Choo hadn't been able to pick up at the neighborhood Rite Aid, and asked him whether he wanted to pay her a visit with me after lunch.

"Of course!" He turned a beaming face to me.

Then I sweetened the pot even more. "Guess the dessert special," I said in my best temptress voice.

Now I had him. He tried to guess, hitting on delicious answers, things I hadn't prepared in quite a while. Nope, nope, and nope. Finally he gave up, his hands on his black-clad hips. "Give," he ordered.

I whispered the forbidden word. "Cannoli."

Landon shrieked, leaped up on a park bench that held only Akahana, and tugged at his hair in full Landon mode, appreciating the brilliance of my move. Then came the inevitable second thoughts. "What if Nonna finds out?" he asked anxiously.

I stood my ground. "How will she find out?" I looked him straight in the eye.

He seemed to consider it; then he erupted gleefully again, fully on board. He'd shave the chocolate. He'd wrap the cannoli tubes. He'd eat the leftovers.

When it looked as if I had dispelled my beloved Landon's mysterious anxiety, I told him I knew he had something on his mind that was troubling him, something about Nonna, and that I wanted to know what it was. I reminded him it was me, Eve, asking, and I enumerated all our shared secrets, appealing to the never-ending twosome of Landon and Eve, the couple that no other couple will ever come between.

He got very quiet. Very collected, for Landon.

Yet he just kept shaking his head. "I can't tell you," he said in a repressed kind of way. I felt completely stymied. Then he took it one step further. "And you can't ask me ever again," he said without a single hint of melodrama.

We stared sorrowfully at each other — I, partly because I felt shut out, but mostly because I couldn't help him. Then my phone rang, its ragtime ringtone feeling jarring at that moment. As I absently reached for it, Landon pressed my arm, murmured something about having to handle this on his own, and turned on his heel.

"Hello," I said, and was surprised to hear Patrick Cahill's voice as I watched my cousin slip away from me.

In more ways than one.

Ten minutes later, I was sitting across from Patrick Cahill with a skinny vanilla latte in my hand. Patrick was drinking something with caramel, chocolate, and cinnamon. Dressed in a beige sport coat and brown polo shirt, he set a folded issue of the *Courier Times* between us on the table. His finger tapped the page 1 photo, and I leaned in. It was the paper from the day after Arlen

Mather's murder: Arlen Mather and Maria Pia having too good a time at the Wine Festival.

"I know this guy," said Patrick.

He had my interest. "Really?"

"Only it says his name is" — with a quick twist of the hand, Patrick had turned the paper around — "Arlen Mather. Is that right?" He looked at me quizzically.

I gave him the full Italian shrug, the one you need a license to perform.

With a swig of his liquid candy shop, Patrick narrowed his eyes at me. "That's not the name he gave me."

"Which was?" I prompted, waiting for Maximiliano to make an appearance.

"Max Scotti."

And there it was.

I was liking it that Patrick had sought me out with this information.

And I wasn't liking it that Dana hadn't.

"Max Scotti," I repeated.

Patrick was nodding. "Right. That's what I knew him as. Dana and I almost hired him."

Now I nodded. "Interior design?" I said knowingly.

Patrick Cahill gave a surprised laugh. "Interior design? I've got Dana for that."

"Right," I said slowly. Topless, bonking,

homicidal Dana.

"You've seen our house. You've seen my office. All Dana. No," Patrick went on, "Max Scotti was a financial adviser."

Now, this was unexpected. "A *financial* adviser?"

"Dana and I were looking to update our portfolio, move some assets around, that sort of thing," he explained.

My idea of moving assets around involved pushing my geranium pots half a foot to the left. "And you hired Max Scotti?"

"No," said Patrick, "we met him socially a couple of times, and we interviewed him. Along with several others. At the time, what with Dana's singing career taking off . . ." He shot me a smile, like the rest was totally understood.

I almost choked on my latte. Dana's *singing* career? We didn't even pay her. She usually referred to her Miracolo gig as "pro bono" work for the good of Quaker Hills.

Patrick had continued, "— so we decided it was time for some professional advice."

"So, Max Scotti?" I managed.

"He seemed qualified from his bona fides, but Dana and I went in another direction. Someone more familiar with vocal artists."

"Of course," I said faintly.

"But the most interesting thing about Max

Scotti had nothing to do with his job. Turns out he was the great-great-nephew of Antonio Scotti, a Metropolitan Opera baritone who sang with Caruso."

Now he had my full attention.

Patrick picked up the folded newspaper. "Not that it matters," he said, "but Max Scotti told me he collected opera memorabilia."

11

Was opera at the bottom of everything happening in Quaker Hills this week?

Murder, saucy photos, disguises, general intrigue, and over-the-top behavior . . . it sure sounded like opera.

I watched Patrick stride up the street to his office, where, any minute now, his glamorous wife would show up in her nondescript skulking outfit. And he'd still think Dana was the dreamiest gal around.

I was due to meet Mrs. Crawford in half an hour, just enough time to pick up the bamboo I had ordered from Flowers by Beck. Where, as it turns out, the long-haired pretty brunette I had spotted a couple of days ago was on duty. In spite of her name tag (OLIVIA How Can I Help You?), I found her to be strangely unhelpful when I tried to draw out the details of her personal life.

All I ended up with was bamboo.

It went marginally better with Mrs. Crawford, whose hot-pink cocktail dress was so loaded with a pattern of peonies, I expected to see ants. In the forty-five minutes we talked alone at Miracolo's bar — she had a gimlet, I had a glass of Chianti — her wide-brimmed, white picture hat didn't come off.

She talked about life as a piano performance student at Berklee.

I talked about life as a dance major at Sarah Lawrence, where Landon's daddy footed the bill.

Then I tried to get all "girlfriendy" and made some opening salvos about dating. Before I came to the conclusion that Mrs. Crawford wasn't going to yield any goodies, I had confessed to a flirtation with an art history professor, an anonymous poem-writing infatuation with a couple of famous actors, and a crush on Maria Pia's Mexican landscaper's son. All Mrs. Crawford gave me was her empty gimlet glass, which I refilled.

When she excused herself to go back to the employee bathroom, I slipped off my shoes and lightly ran after her. Through the dining room, through the kitchen, into the short back hallway leading to the office. The door to the john was closed, and since the door was a bit too short, there was a generous gap at the bottom.

My plan to solve the gender mystery of Mrs. Crawford was simple, as every brilliant plan should be. Ply her with beverages. Follow her to the bathroom. Perform surveillance of the crack. When I saw where her pumps were located, I'd have my answer.

If I saw toes, she's a female.

If I saw heels, she's a male.

I silently stretched out along the floor, and just as I turned my neck into viewing position, I heard a voice right behind me. "What are you doing?"

With all my might, I pushed myself up and opened outward into a side plank, sending my arm skyward. Considering I had never pulled off that yoga pose with anything like grace, I was doing a pretty fair job at it. "Speaks for itself, doesn't it?" I cast a sideways glance at the voice, which turned out to belong to Joe Beck.

At that moment the bathroom door opened and Mrs. Crawford nearly fell over me. "Oh, my, you surprised me," she laughed in a breathy baritone way, holding up her hands. "What are you doing there?"

"Side plank." How much longer could I hold this pose?

Joe gave me a flat look. "I guess that clears up one mystery."

"But not all the mysteries," I managed to get out.

The difference in the way we all see things is what makes the world work: we mainly stymie each other just long enough to keep off murder. It's only when we understand each other completely that we get into trouble — like when we know we both want the same X square miles of land, or the same pitcher who throws 103 mph fastballs, or the same sweet-smelling, day-trading Marlboro Man.

As a tool for peace, human misunderstanding is seriously underrated.

Mrs. Crawford thought Joe was hitting on me. Joe thought I was spying on Mrs. Crawford. (The fact that he was right is irrelevant.) And I thought Mrs. Crawford had made it her perverse mission to confound me.

After our piano player left I headed for the front door, figuring Joe would probably follow. He did.

"Two things," he announced.

"Oh?"

"Olivia tells me you left your Visa at the flower shop."

"Olivia?" I feigned disinterest.

"My brother's wife."

Once we were on the sidewalk, I locked

Miracolo. "What's the second thing?" I asked.

He rubbed the back of his very lovely neck. "There's been another robbery in the commercial district."

Oh no! "Where? Who?"

"Frantiques," he said with a wince.

Fran Beller was the owner of an antiques shop two blocks south of Market Square. Nice gal, good customer. "When?"

"Sometime last night," he told me. "The alarm was disabled and the back door was jimmied open. Ted and Sally are still over there."

"What was taken?" I asked.

"Couple of folk art pieces, couple of Madame Alexander dolls, a Baccarat vase, Victorian necklaces, some candlesticks. I forget what else."

I shook my head. "I feel bad for Fran."

"Just keep Miracolo locked up tight," he said, then tweaked my chin. I was beginning to think he was hitting on me, and I flushed.

He went on, "Actually, three."

"Three what?"

"Can't you keep up?" he teased. "Plank get to you, Angelotta? Three things."

What an annoying man. "What's the third?"

Maddeningly, Joe started to walk up the street.

"What's the third?" I yelled after him.

He looked back at me with a grin, but kept walking. "The answer is" — he entered the flower shop — "female."

Which was precisely when my ringtone warbled at me, preventing the enormously clever and witty retort I'm sure I would have thought of.

It was Tony Treadwell, and after our hellos, he got down to business. "I've heard back from our field operative, Veronica Gale," he reported.

"Lay it on me," I told him, excited.

"She called someone she knows at ASID headquarters and spun some tale about a possible design job for member Arlen Mather."

"Good one," I breathed with respect.

"That's Veronica."

I prompted him, "And?"

"Well, on this score, at least, your Mr. Mather was not a stand-up kind of guy. According to her source, no one named Arlen Mather has ever belonged to ASID."

It's funny how dead ends baffle you when it comes to the information you think you wanted . . . but then they round out a completely different picture. The man called Arlen Mather was setting himself up in what looked like a new life, credentials or no. *Who was he, really?* And what, besides the obvious, did he want with Nonna?

I thanked him and hung up as the Tri-State Linen Supply truck pulled up, and the driver started unloading our order. Arne was inhumanly punctual. And because he was so Austrian and sincere, I didn't want to disabuse him of his belief in my reverence for the almighty clock. This was never an easy thing, because we Angelottas run a bit on Northern Italian Time, which is somewhat closer to Greenwich Mean Time than Southern Italian Time, thanks to years of interbreeding with our marauding neighbors from the Tyrol, whose raids, you can bet, went like clockwork.

Arne shouldered the big white cotton bags and traipsed after me into the restaurant, where I stepped aside and let him flop the load onto the booth at the back. Arne was strong and grim and thin-haired, and I often found myself hoping he secretly collected Beatrix Potter miniatures or something. He gave me his deep nod, which signaled that that was it until next time, and held out the clipboard. Neither of us had a pen, so we went into the kitchen.

Arne and Eve. The perfect relationship: ten minutes twice a week. No wine, chat, or love tokens. Arne always made me mist up with gratitude.

Rummaging around in the junk drawer, I found a pen and scribbled my signature on Arne's neatly clipped paperwork. After I dropped the pen back into the drawer, Arne grunted and headed toward the front door as I looked out the kitchen window.

And saw Dana.

Upstairs at the photographer's again.

What in the ding-dong doo-wop shim-sham was the woman doing?

At least she appeared to be fully clothed.

While I kept half an eye on her, I pulled the washed, starched, pressed, and folded white table linens out of the oversize cotton bags. Suddenly I saw Dana walk out of sight, so I hightailed it into the dining room, where I piled the tablecloths on the booth and left the empty bags on top.

As she emerged onto the street, I charged through the front door at Miracolo, quickly locked up, and caught up with her just outside Sprouts. She was dressed in a ruffled white T-shirt, black capris, a red leather bag with enough gold chains to give Houdini a run for his money, and gold lamé slides. Just as it was registering with her that

I had her by the elbow, I said in a cheery voice, "Okay, Dana, let's talk."

She was blinking and smiling. Bad poker player. "What's this —"

I propelled us both through the traffic on North Market Square and headed into the park. Out of earshot of the Mom Brigade near the playground, I let her go and got pretty much in her face. "What's going on?"

I expected *Whaddya mean?,* forgetting how formal Dana gets whenever she's cornered. What I got was, "Whatever are you talking about?" Suddenly the Southern belle who never lived any farther south than Asbury Park, New Jersey.

"I saw you at Pixie Pix."

"I was — visiting a friend," she answered airily.

"Topless?" I raised my eyebrows. "Must be a very good friend."

She blurted, "How did you —"

"You were standing in the window, Dana."

"I was changing," she told me with dignity. "In a changing room, Miss Nibby Nose." Miss Nibby Nose? "I'm having some portraits taken." I could see the wheels turn quickly. "For Patrick," she flung at me, practically euphoric at the lie.

I let it sit for a minute; then I hit her with, "Why were you sneaking into Jolly's?"

She gasped, and turned it into a fake cough. Then the Southern belle was back. "You don't know all my friends, Eve. Sometimes I visit Roland —"

I gave her a flat look. "Reginald. So you sneak in the back?"

"Patrick is jealous," she confided, like she was telling me he wore pink garters.

Okay, that was lower than a crawdad on a river bottom, laying it on poor Patrick. "Oh, Dana, cut it out. Reginald Jolly didn't even know your name when I asked him about the key."

She wouldn't budge. "That's no—"

"Just tell me the truth," I said, making my point with a little push on her shoulder. "I had a dead body in my kitchen and now my nonna's in jail, and I'm unlocking the doors of Hell by putting cannoli on the specials board, so don't mess around with me, girlfriend." She had the good sense to back up. "I'm a desperado, you got that?"

She whispered, "I can't help you."

"From what I can tell" — I started ticking off her sins on my fingers — "you have no alibi for the morning of the murder, you're posing topless for skank shots, and you're up to something at Jolly's Pub. Unless you want me to run this information by Patrick, you're going to come clean with me." I looked at my watch. "And right now. Because I have to get to the jail."

"You're mean," she hissed.

"If I were mean, I'd tell you how to sing 'You're So Vain.' " I immediately felt bad, and wished I could take it back.

She exploded: "Well, Eloise Timmler at Le Chien Rouge loved it! Loved it, Eve, when I sang it for *her.*"

Now completely perplexed, I asked, "Why are you singing for Eloise Timmler?"

"Why do you think?" Dana looked me straight in the eye. "I auditioned for her."

"Auditioned? For what?"

"For a singing gig!" she practically yelled.

I was mystified. "You've got a singing gig."

"Eve," she said in a dose-of-reality tone of voice, "I'm not going to stay at Miracolo forever. I owe it to my talent to look for bigger and better venues."

"Full of *Crêpe*?" It was half the size of Miracolo and totally cheesy. "So that's where you were the morning of the murder?"

She heaved a frustrated sigh. "I didn't want to tell you before I knew I got the gig. Then I'd give you two weeks' notice."

There was now one less suspect in Arlen Mather's murder, but I felt lighter than air. I was Gene Kelly swinging around that streetlight with a hundred-watt smile, imagining late night at Miracolo, without the "soulful stylings" of my pal. We might actually draw some new customers.

Suddenly I realized — "Jolly's! You auditioned for Reginald, too, didn't you?"

"Well, all he wanted was a head shot and CV."

Reginald was smooth and canny enough to figure a way out of hiring her.

"So you went to Pixie Pix."

She nodded. "Jolly's, of course, is the primo place in town."

This was news to me, because *Zagat* and I agreed that Miracolo was. But Dana always believes that the thing she's going to is so much better than the thing she's leaving — which, of course, was so much better than the thing she left before that.

"But right now he's not hiring," she said sadly.

"And Eloise Timmler?"

Dana grabbed my arms and gave me such a look of excitement that I almost laughed. "She's letting me know today." Dana pressed a hand to her chest. "I'd get to sing Piaf!" Then her voice dropped. "You know how I so identify with the Little French Wren."

Sparrow, but what the hell.

The minute she took a gig at Full of Crêpe was the minute I'd have to let her go, friends or no. The only thing worse than Dana exposed was Dana overexposed. In a town the size of Quaker Hills, it would never do. But how could I tell her and still save the friendship?

Landon got into the Volvo in a muffled, muzzled mood. I scrutinized him. He was actually wearing his dad's old powder-blue warm-up suit from 1985. He has always been of the opinion that powder blue washes him out, and he was right. The last time one of those moods hit he bought a Barcalounger. In brown.

I stared at him, but he looked unblinkingly ahead. "Jonathan should only see you," I said.

"Just drive," he countered.

I obeyed. "Are you in one of your 'We're All Going to Die' moods? Or one of your 'There's Got to Be More to Life Than Italian Cooking' moods?"

He inhaled. "Both," he said finally.

Truly serious, then. "Explain." I rounded a corner, leading us out of the commercial district.

He tucked his nice chin into his chest. "We're all going to die, but I don't want

Nonna to be first."

"You don't?" I was flabbergasted. "I do. Much as I love her, she damn well *should* be first, Landon."

"Not this way," he said, shooting me a look. "Not in prison."

My teeth worked the inside of my cheek. "What else?"

"Yes, there's more to life than Italian cooking," he burst out, "but with Nonna gone, what does it —"

"Okay, wait just a minute. You've already got her tried and convicted, Landon. So she dropped Arlen Mather off at the restaurant that morning. So she lied about picking up the dress at Saks. So she doesn't have an alibi worth a damn. It'll be okay. You'll see."

When he said, "I'm going to Hell," his eyes all glazed and puffy, I swiftly pulled over and shifted into Park.

"Landon, you don't even believe in Hell."

"I don't believe in gay bars, either, but I go there." He huddled against the car door, looking smaller than I could stand.

"Hardly the same, Landon." I rubbed the back of his neck. "Hardly the same." Then: "*Caro mio,* tell me what's wrong." He just kept sighing. Finally, I released my seat belt and wrapped my arms around his shoulders. "Landon."

197

We sat together in silence for a few minutes.

"I don't want to make it your problem, too," he mumbled.

I peered into his stricken face. "Hey, I'm making cannoli tonight, so I'm already going to Hell if Nonna ever finds out."

He laughed softly.

"You can only make it my problem if you *don't* tell me, *capisce*?"

He nodded slightly and seemed to come to some conclusion. "You remember the morning of the murder?" he said, pulling away just enough to face me. I nodded. "Remember when I came into the kitchen?" Of course. "Well, before I got to the kitchen, I found something in the dining room, Eve."

"Go on."

The words tumbled out. "I was going to show you, but then the murder kind of took over. And then later, I found it in my pocket, where I must have shoved it. Not thinking, you know?" His eyes pleaded for understanding. "And I just kept staring at it, because suddenly I knew what it meant, and I just couldn't bring myself to take it to the cops."

Now I was worried. "Landon, honey, what is it?"

Very slowly, from the baggy pocket of his

powder-blue warm-up suit, my cousin Landon pulled something shiny. A silver bracelet. He opened his hand all the way, so I could look at it. The clasp was broken.

"I found it on the dining room floor, right near the kitchen doors."

We both stared at the bracelet, and then at each other.

It was the twenty-fifth anniversary present from our grandfather to his wife, Maria Pia. "It could have fallen off anytime," I said reasonably.

Landon slowly shook his head, looking at me with something like pity. "I checked, Eve. The cleaning crew had been there during the night. They would have seen it. She dropped it that morning. She didn't just drop Arlen Mather off. She went inside, Eve."

The question was, why?

12

"Withholding evidence," I said into my phone in a purely hypothetical sort of way.

"Yes?" said Joe Beck warily.

"What can you tell me about it?" Beside me, Landon was chewing a fingernail.

Joe rattled off, "Spoliation of evidence means altering, destroying —"

"Wait, wait," I said with a laugh, "who said anything about spoliating?"

The man plowed on. "Covering up, concealing . . ."

I suppose that part included stuffing the evidence absentmindedly into one's pocket. And showing it three days later to one's cousin. "Okay, I got the picture. How bad are we talking here?"

Silence. Then: "What are you withholding?" Then: "No, don't tell me. I don't want to know."

My voice dropped. "I don't blame you."

After about three seconds, he went on:

"I've still got your Visa, so I want you to authorize a one-dollar charge."

I was puzzled. "What for?"

"Me."

"Don't you think that's a little high?" I couldn't resist.

"Quit kidding around," said Joe a trifle sternly. "You're hiring me."

Did the bottom drop out of the lawyer market? "I thought you charge four hundred an hour."

"That's when I actually do something for the money. For a buck, you've just bought yourself attorney-client privilege."

I already liked the sound of it. "Which means?"

"You can tell me your deepest, darkest secrets and I can legally keep my trap shut."

I reached for my secret stash of pico de gallo chips, tucked away in the glove compartment. "Okay, Joe, I authorize you to put a buck on my card." Then I turned to Landon. "Now I've got me a lawyer."

Landon looked encouraging, and pointed to himself.

I turned back to the phone. "For another buck, can you be Landon's, too?"

"Whatever. Yes. Fine."

"Now, about those consequences." I filled him in on Landon's finding the bracelet and stuffing it into his pocket until now.

By that point, Joe Beck was groaning. "No, no, no, no . . ."

Wasn't looking good. "So tell me."

"Up to twenty years."

I needed to hear some wiggle room. "Hypothetically?"

He got a bit starchy. "There's nothing hypothetical about prison, Eve, so if you —"

"Thanks, Joe." If he was going to go all Marian the Librarian on me, he was useless.

"Wait!" He raised his voice. "None of that's going to happen, because you're going to take that bracelet to Ted and Sally. Right now. And you're going to —"

"Thanks, Joe, talk to you later." I hung up as we pulled up to the two-story brick colonial that housed the Quaker Hills Police Department. Landon grabbed his canvas tote with Bad-Ass Tree Hugger scrawled across it that contained some goodies for Maria Pia: a box of Godiva dark chocolates, her blue kimono, a few *People* magazines, new red rhinestone reading glasses, a pump container of Lubriderm, and a Magic 8 Ball.

I slipped the bracelet into my purse, the bauble that could buy Landon and me twenty years in the slammer. I needed time to think.

Inside, the QHPD was surprisingly bright and pretty nonthreatening, considering. Hanging globe lamps, natural woodwork, those little white octagonal floor tiles. Through a half-glass wall near the back, I saw Ted downing an overstuffed sub at his desk.

The desk sergeant signed us in and escorted us to the door at the back, which led to the cells. All two of them. Nonna sat on the edge of her lower bunk, a thin green blanket wrapped like a pashmina around her shoulders. Her hair was flopped in all the wrong directions and yesterday's mascara had slid off her lashes. She looked every one of her seventy-six years, and I hated it.

The desk sergeant settled into a chair near the entrance and started rummaging through our Bad-Ass Tree Hugger bag, checking, I suppose, for metal files.

I heard Landon swallow a squeak, so I wrapped an arm around his waist. "Not a word about the cannoli," I whispered.

He glanced at me quickly. "It would kill her — what's left of her."

"Same with the bracelet." Then brightly: "Hi, Nonna!"

"Nonna?" Landon cajoled her.

We moved in close at the door of her cell,

our hands gripping the bars. She finally looked up at us blankly; then she rushed over and kissed our fingers, the only part of us she could easily reach, which was pretty sweet. "Tell me, tell me, how is my Miracolo?"

Landon fielded that one. "Fine, Nonna. Lots of customers —"

"Some gawkers," I put in, just to be truthful.

"Eve's brilliant food," gushed Landon. I tried to look modest. He added: "And Mrs. Crawford is on fire at the piano."

Then I remembered. "Dana dedicated 'Three Coins in the Fountain' to you," I told her, rubbing her hands, which were clutching the bars.

Nonna sniffled, clearly moved. "That girl can hardly sing, but *she* is a dear, considerate child with a heart as big as a *zuppa inglese* —"

I definitely didn't imagine that emphasis. "*She* is auditioning for gigs all over town."

"That *strega!*" she breathed. Maria Pia suddenly looked as good as if she had spent the last four hours in a spa. Then she told us she had hired Belinda DiMaio to represent her.

I told her that that idiot Belinda DiMaio couldn't defend her decision to go to law school, let alone anyone charged with murder. Then I got bossy and told Nonna that she already had a lawyer: mine.

Landon gaped at me.

"He will accompany you to the arraignment." *Note to self: Call Joe.* "And I'll call off Belinda."

Nonna twisted her hankie, her earnest eyes on my face. "Well, that — that thing you just said —"

"The arraignment?"

"It's been postponed. Someone got the flu."

Quaker Hills: three cops, two cells, one judge. For the first time since I had left Manhattan, I felt like I had moved to Mayberry.

Landon and I gave each other a quick look. This was Friday, and Maria Pia didn't seem to have absorbed the implications. She was a jailbird for the whole weekend now.

"Choo Choo says you have" — I glanced back up the corridor to where the desk sergeant was snoozing, and whispered anyway — "something to confess."

Maria Pia dropped her hands from the bars and gazed heavenward with a pious look. I knew she was referencing her favorite paintings of the Blessed Virgin Mary, where her eyes are rolled up to the corner of the

205

room and she looks like she's thinking, *This kid is driving me crazy.*

"I do." She chewed her lower lip. We waited. Landon looked like he was going to topple over with suspense. Finally: "I went back," she breathed, her eyes still heavenward.

"You went back?"

"That morning."

"Of the murder?"

She blew. Ten seconds of piety is just about her limit. "Of course, of the murder!" She glared at me. "What have we been talking about? My poor dead Arlen —"

"Whose real name, by the way, was Maximiliano Scotti," I inserted.

Nonna looked as befuddled as she had at her arrest. Then she got instantly to the most essential piece of the new information. "You mean he was Italian?"

I could read the unspoken thoughts that darted vividly across her face: she always knew there was something she liked about him; her boyfriend had just been revealed to be the lost prince of an obscenely wealthy kingdom; how particularly sad the world has lost such a fine example of an Italian; she will never love again.

"Yes, Italian, Nonna," I said. "And a financial adviser."

We then covered, in conspiratorial whis-
pers, many crazy-making points in the case.
She had gone back to Miracolo maybe an
hour after she dropped Arlen/Max off, and
discovered his body. (This at least explained
the loss of the silver bracelet. It also put her
right on the scene during the key times.)

She couldn't explain the change of identity
problem, from Max to Arlen. Not a clue. I
wasn't totally inclined to believe her. After
all, I'd believed her all those years ago when
she told me my father had gone on a two-
year scientific mission to the Amazon to find
new edible greens; then, two years later,
when he didn't turn up, she had to produce
the famous farewell note.

Okay, so about Max Scotti, great-great-
nephew of a famous baritone, opera aficio-
nado and collector, and financial adviser,
okay, maybe she knew nothing.

But how could she know *nothing* about
Arlen Mather, he of the bogus ties to the
famous sermonizing Puritan family? From
what I'd heard of the guy, Arlen didn't seem
too concerned with the state of his immortal
soul.

I handed her his business card and saw a
flicker of fear on her face.

"Where did you get this?"

"From Kayla."

"Kayla?" She was incredulous. Was this man's business card such a rarity?

It seemed to be the time to tell Maria Pia the truth about Arlen Mather and her great-niece. "Arlen dumped her for you."

More flights of facial expressions, all unspoken: oh that dear sweet man; I have powers the likes of which you can only dream of; I have bested a *bella ragazza* forty years younger than my glorious self.

"Did you know about his interior design business?"

"Of course I knew. Why do you think I hired him?" she finished with a bold toss of her uncombed hair.

"You hired him?" This was Landon.

"You hired an interior designer?" This was me.

Sometimes the long, slow, dark road suddenly comes slamming right up to you as a shorter, faster, darker one, complete with a brick wall. My heart started pounding harder than when Ted and Sally had shown up at Miracolo with a warrant for her arrest.

What I felt then was fear. This was something else.

"Yes," Nonna said defensively, "I hired an interior designer."

"What for?" Landon still didn't see it.

208

Maria Pia had the good sense to step back from the bars of her cell, where my hands couldn't reach her. "You can look at me like that all you want, Eve," she said softly, "but it doesn't change the facts."

"And what are those?" I said flatly.

Queen Maria Pia made an appearance. "I hired Arlen Mather to redecorate Miracolo." It all came tumbling out. She had dropped him off that morning to look over the space with a view toward covering up those hideous old brick walls with lovely red-flocked wallpaper — here Landon gasped — and paintings of Mount Vesuvius, with maybe some little niches for reproductions of David and Cupid and Venus and Caesar, and maybe a *fontana* up front near the cash register —

I suddenly understood how my precious Caruso recording of "Your Eyes Have Told Me What I Did Not know" had wound up under the body. Arlen/Max had started to take down the shadow boxes to get a better look at the walls.

My eyes got dangerously narrow. "When were you planning on telling me?"

She gave me a sideways glance. "I was planning it as a *sorpresa.*" A surprise.

My Crap Detector was going *ding, ding, ding, ding.* "When were you planning on having the work done?"

Queen Maria Pia stood taller. Her chin lifted. "In June."

And then I saw it all. "When I'd be in Orlando?"

She'd planned to send me to the American Culinary Federation's annual convention just to get me out of the way so she could tart up our precious restaurant until you couldn't tell it from any other Italian restaurant from fifty years ago. It was diabolical. It would be disastrous.

"Nonna!" said Landon with profound disappointment.

I got right up in her face. "Mather was a liar, Nonna."

"What are you talking about?" Haughty to the max.

"He wasn't really a member of the American Society of Interior Designers."

A flicker on her face told me she hadn't known. Then: "It doesn't matter, Miss Priss. He knew what he was doing. You don't know anything!"

She stood in her cell looking stubborn and righteous, and I considered letting Belinda DiMaio defend her after all. That was as close to a *malocchio* as I could get — and probably more effective. But I needed something *now* . . .

"Guess what I'm making for the dessert special this evening, Nonna?" I started to walk away, then turned and looked her straight in the eye. "Cannoli."

To the sounds of *molto* agitation, I tugged at Landon's sleeve and swept past the dozing desk sergeant.

I dropped Landon back off at his place, where he declared he needed a lot of cuddle time with his cat, the mighty Vaughn, before coming to work. Then I headed over to my tiny house, where I changed into my new red summer sheath and black sandals for my at-long-last "work date" at Miracolo with Mark Metcalf.

I couldn't let my mind wander in the direction of my treacherous grandmother. No wonder the Ancient Roman Empire collapsed: they slathered red-flocked wallpaper on everything and thought it was *bellissimo*. And don't even get me started on the Mount Vesusius and Lake Como schlock.

Maybe I'd call Joe, maybe not.

Maybe I'd turn in the silver bracelet, maybe not.

Maybe I'd fire Dana, maybe not.

Maybe I'd get a restraining order against Maria Pia, keeping her fifty yards away from Miracolo, maybe not.

One thing was for sure: I was making cannoli. With a vengeance.

As I swung myself back into the Volvo, I was pondering Arlen/Max's change of identity. It's one thing to change your career. It's another thing to change your name. What had Maximiliano Scotti done that he wanted to change both? And why was he killed at our restaurant? What about Miracolo or Quaker Hills made the killer strike *there*? It's not as though Quaker Hills was a hotbed of —

But wait a minute.

It *was* a hotbed of crime. There were all those thefts over the last three months. The rug shop, two antique stores. And "Arlen Mather" was an interior designer. Was there any connection between those robberies . . . and his murder?

It was such a delicious possibility that by the time I pulled onto Market Square, I felt like I fit the very cool red summer sheath I was wearing. Red, as we all know, is a state of mind. And in my current state of mind, the game plan was to disarm and seduce Mark Metcalf. I'd had enough of my nonna's conniving, enough of Arlen/Max's murder, and enough of kissless good-nights on the run.

Ah, that wonderful midday feel at Miracolo. Nothing like it. The pale light sifting through the blinds always makes me think of the word *lambent.* The light slanted and hung dancing in the air of the dining room, like even the dust was waiting for love. I confess I peeked into Miracolo's office and eyed the saddle-brown leather couch that should have sported crime scene tape, what with the crime against sense and taste committed by Joe and Kayla. Well . . . not to mention me and the FedEx man.

Landon wasn't due until 2 p.m., so there was plenty of time for some love in the afternoon with Mark. I was even feeling soft toward Frank Sinatra — maybe a little "Strangers in the Night" wouldn't be amiss? With a quick check that the front door was unlocked, I walked back to the double doors to the kitchen, glancing at the pile of linens still flopped onto the booth. Feeling incredibly hot in my red dress that knew just where to cling without appearing needy, I entered the kitchen lost in precouch reveries. And then I got bagged.

With a swoop, one of Arne's big white cotton delivery bags came down over my head and tightened around my knees, pulling me literally off my feet. I let out a strangled whoop, hitting out like a deranged mime. What was happening? "Cut it out!

Cut it out!" I kept yelling, scratching at the stifling fabric like my stubby fingernails were going to get me out of the bag.

And then I got double-bagged. The hands were big and fast, pulling a second bag up over my kicking feet, winding the pull cord around me like a mummy. When I got lifted up, I started screaming. Before I knew what was happening, I was tumbled someplace close to the kitchen and a door was shut firmly behind me. I wasn't hit with Arctic air, so it wasn't the walk-in fridge. There was a scraping sound as something got jammed against the doorknob.

Then, silence.

Someone was having his way with my restaurant. True, better it than me. But still.

I struggled, feeling a whole lot like Harry Houdini trying to slip magically out of a straitjacket. I stopped long enough to inchworm my way across the floor to see if I could figure out my space. My bagged black-sandaled feet struck something, so I experimentally kicked out hard. Metal. When my feet made out large round cylinders, I knew I'd hit upon the bottom shelf of the storeroom, where we kept megajugs of imported olive oil.

Was there anything here that could help me?

I tried to picture the space. Any kitchen utensils? Scissors? Cutlery? Even if I'd landed in a scissors factory, I didn't see how I was even going to be able to get to my feet.

Out of frustration, I started to growl. I had cannoli to make — Maria Pia–defying cannoli. If my hands weren't immobilized against my thighs, I'd shake my fists. With these developments, I was going to run out of time both for a frolic with Mark and a decent shot at making my dessert special. Could this day possibly get any worse?

And then I got mad.

I kicked at the seams of the bag, finally punching out a hole. It was all I could do to fold myself in half, reaching down, down, down with my grasping hands to the place where I'd torn the bag. Then I ripped with a vengeance, tearing apart the inner bag. From there it was just a matter of time before I'd torn through the outer bag and pulled apart the tied cords. When I was bag free, I inventoried myself, noting the sore left side of my body from being pulled off my feet, noting the big hanks of hair that were crisscrossed in every direction like some of the worst bad hair I'd ever seen.

Red dress: intact.

Then I started pounding with my fists on

the jammed door. "Help!" Sometimes I took a turn hammering with my forearms. "Help!" Every so often I tugged like a madwoman at the doorknob. Nothing. I kept yelling for help at the top of my lungs like I was trying to get out of some circle of Hell even Dante didn't know about.

Half an hour, a full hour, the month of June . . . who knows how long I was trapped there? All I could do was yell. And, I have to admit, cry a little bit.

Suddenly I heard a voice, far off.

Someone was calling my name. Then the voice got closer. "Eve?"

Joe! My heart lifted right up.

"Here!" I screamed. "In here!"

"Where are you?"

I called again, pounding with all my might on the door: "In here! I'm locked in!"

Then the chair that was jamming the doorknob was sliding away. I took a step back. My sandals were scuffed from the struggle, my hair was heading off in three different demented directions, my tearstained mascara was giving Maria Pia's a run for the money, and one hand was gripping the opposite shoulder, which was throbbing from the fall. Just as the door swung open, I realized that one side of the hem of my dress had managed to lodge itself in my underpants.

I was, in short, a vision.

And standing there before me, was . . . Mark Metcalf.

13

My disappointment was unreasonable. I should have been happy to see anybody, right? But Joe made such a nice cup of tea that, while locked in the storeroom, I found myself wondering what he was like in a clinch — strictly in the sense of dicey circumstances, you understand. Still, there was that dimple, and that smile that seemed to come from someplace the sun only dreams about. Was I actually attracted to the guy?

"What's going on?" said Mark. Apparently Real Marlboro Men get baffled by things like picking up their dates in storerooms.

Darting past him, I said, "I'm not sure," and freed the hem of my dress as I headed for the office. "Did you see anybody?" I threw back at him, walking in dizzy circles in the room where we keep all our files — and our safe. It's really just a "show" safe from back in my great-grandfather's day, when he used to keep the day's receipts in it. Now it was an antique piece of furniture with a faded white lace doily and a foot-high porcelain clown playing a violin on it. Inside were my old report cards and the boxed ashes of Maria Pia's beloved dachshund, Carmen, who died back in 1974. No cash, but no one else knew that.

The safe was untouched.

"No, I didn't see anyone," Mark said, scratching his chin.

"I was jumped," I told him. "Don't touch anything." The office looked undisturbed, which was more than I could say for myself. I still had to see the worst of whatever had just happened in my restaurant.

"So I'm guessing this isn't a good time," he said, trying for humor.

"Probably not," I said in a tight voice, not even looking at him. In one of those acts you can't explain, like saving a cloth napkin out of a tornado-flattened home, I stopped by the storeroom and grabbed the two delivery sacks used on me and started to fold them with shaking hands. *Call the cops,* came that same little know-it-all voice that bothers us with admonitions like *Don't forget to floss.* Where was my purse? Where was my phone? Could I just scream "911! 911!"

at the top of my lungs and have someone appear?

He moved in really close. "Can I help you?" he asked, his hand touching my bare arm.

All I could do was shake my head wordlessly.

Then, spying my purse on the counter just inside the double doors, I pushed the linens bags at Mark and found my phone. I saw it was 1:34 p.m. As I dialed 911, I stepped into the dining room and my breath caught in my throat. The walls were bare. All the shadow boxes had been taken down.

I dashed around the room while I told the dispatcher we had been robbed. The boxes had been pried open and left empty on the floor. I was stunned. Into the phone, I added, "And I was locked up."

With Mark at my side, I stood in the center of Miracolo and surveyed the place. All of my opera memorabilia was gone. Galli-Curci's fan from *Madama Butterfly*. Titta Ruffo's ruff from *Ernani*. The demo record of Beniamino Gigli singing "Goodbye, Marie." The prop dagger from the Met's production of *Otello*. Rosa Ponselle's corset from *Aida*. The jar of spirit gum used to attach Caruso's mustache in *Rigoletto*. And the gloves he had worn.

It suddenly felt as if all of my friends had been kidnapped, and I was left alone.

Since Mark couldn't help me, I sent him on his way. We went back and forth — *Are you sure? Yes, I'm sure* — a couple of times, but finally I prevailed. He told me he'd call. I'd told him I'd answer the phone.

So all I spent was a bad seven and a half minutes by myself until Sally and Ted showed up, eyeballing me, the wreckage, and each other, as if they just knew the theft had something to do with the murder of Arlen Mather. Today Sally was wearing a candy-striped shirt with a silver belt over a raspberry-colored pencil skirt and silver shoes. I would have paid money to watch her chase after the thief in that footwear.

"So," she drawled, flipping open her battered notebook, "lay it on me."

As I described what had happened, I started shaking, but I couldn't tell whether it was anger or a delayed reaction to being scared stiff.

By the time Sally and Ted were done taking my statement and inventorying the stolen items, Landon arrived, singing Billy Joel's "Movin' Out" in his Broadway voice. Until he got a load of Quaker Hills's finest.

"Landon," I said, my voice shaking, "we've

been robbed. All of my stuff is gone."

Speechless, he took in the blank brick walls with a gasp, then the empty shadow boxes.

Sally and Ted packed it in, saying they'd send the crime scene team to dust for prints — yes, we could open for dinner tonight — and then left.

After I showed Landon the storeroom and he was properly horrified, he did the one thing I could not: he slipped into his white chef's jacket and started to make cannoli. He was all business, and I was all inertia.

While Landon filled the deep fryer with oil and started to mix the ingredients for cannoli dough, I called Joe. He was in a monosyllabic mood, but I was too gob-smacked by the theft to care.

"We were robbed," I said dramatically.

All I got was, "Huh."

I waved a hand he couldn't see. "All my opera memorabilia is gone!"

"That's a shame."

Was that the best he could do? "And I was attacked," I disclosed in the voice eight-year-olds use when they've been chased home from school by a big scary dog.

"No!"

"Yes! I was bagged and stuffed in the storeroom."

Here he mumbled. At first, it sounded like "Wish I'd thought of it," but then I realized it was "Wow," although it held a whiff of sarcasm.

Then I got to the point: "My nonna has hired Belinda DiMaio, of all people."

A thoughtful "Hmm," followed by "Bad."

I let out a sigh. "Are you on a daily word quota or something?"

He made a noncommittal noise.

I crossed my eyes at Landon, who was sifting flour like he was panning for gold. Then I asked the critical question: "Will you represent her instead?"

A beat. "Sure."

"Someone got sick so the arraignment's not until early next week." That should interest him.

"That's tough." He sounded sincere. "What happens then?"

"Charges," he said airily, "then bail."

"Good. That's good."

As I watched Landon perform his signature one-handed egg-crack, I found myself feeling bad about Joe for some dim reason. A reason I had left behind, before being bagged and locked up taught me that I was a definite hindrance to somebody.

"Do I owe you an apology?" I asked him.

"Word," spoken in a tone of voice that said

You must have ricotta stuffed up your nose. Practically Italian. I was oddly touched.

I winced, remorseful. "Is it the hanging up on you, before?"

"Partly."

"I'm sorry, Joe, I really am." The guy had been nothing but nice. "So . . . we're good?"

His silence was not encouraging. Finally: "Bracelet?"

I sagged, wishing he hadn't remembered. "Not yet," I had to tell him in a tight little voice.

He snorted.

Watching Landon measure out the sugar, I made my case to my lawyer. "Listen, Joe, my nonna didn't kill that guy. But if I give that bracelet to Sally and Ted, they're going to stop looking for the real killer —"

"Twenty years, Eve."

"We'll find the real killer, and then the bracelet won't matter." Umm . . . that sounded a lot like the gang on Scooby-Doo.

"You'll get sprung just in time to enjoy menopause."

And then I think I flipped out just a little. Landon turned to me, alarmed, with a bottle of Soave in one hand and a measuring cup in the other. I blithered into the phone to Joe about a crazy grandmother who's lying about finding dead bodies and decorating behind my back, a bunch of tarantella dancers rehearsing behind my back, a diva who's interviewing behind my back for a better gig that doesn't even exist, and then the date I had *really* been looking forward to today went right up in smoke, despite my sizzling red dress, and if Joe knew what was good for him, he had better not say a *word* about the office couch.

Finally, he spoke. "Done?"

"I'm not sure," I said belligerently.

"You had a hot date?"

"With Mark Metcalf, yes," I said. "But now I look like a loser who can't even manage not to get jumped in her own restaurant."

"Well, if he's a good guy . . ." he said, barely audible.

"He's a great guy. A day trader," I added, trying to sound like I knew what that was. "We've already been out a couple of times, and I think this could really go somewhere." God, I sounded like I was having a smoky late-night chat with college girlfriends.

"Well, great." If words could sound like a shrug, his did. Then his voice changed and he sounded all buttoned up and buttoned down, telling me he was calling a meeting of the Free Maria Pia "operatives" for Saturday morning at eleven at his place.

Time to check in on any new developments in the investigation.

"Okay, good," I said, writing down the address.

"On the subject of any new evidence of the spoliated variety," he said in a testy voice, "nothing will be said."

"I understand."

Landon turned on the mixer and stood over it watchfully. About cannoli, I had taught him everything I know.

I went on, "You've probably got plans tonight, but we could use your help if you feel like stopping by. Once all this settles down I'll make you anything on the menu, paired with any wine you like, on the house." Eve Angelotta: prefers crow served with milanese sauce.

"Probably not."

"Oh." My cheeks burned. "Okay." To get to this level of rejection, you'd need earth-moving equipment.

"Thanks anyway," he said. "I'll go see Maria Pia."

And he hung up. Probably off to do something behind my back, which apparently was where everything worth doing happened.

There was no getting around it. Whatever slight charm I used to have was now in short supply. Maybe it had been sautéed, steamed, and simmered right out of me over the last few years here in — let's face it — what was really Maria Pia's kitchen. Maybe I'd just left it behind in Manhattan, along with all the dreams that mattered. Say what you will about the rents, in New York I never discovered dead bodies, never needed a lawyer, never got jumped and bagged.

Had the last three years been a colossal mistake? Had I been hiding out?

Just when I was feeling like this was a question of somewhat more importance than when Choo Choo was going to get there with the fish for the *fritto misto di pesce,* Choo Choo showed up with the fish. He was growing a goatee, and his new shirt was a sexy shade of blue-violet and didn't seem so Big and Tall as usual. And then I realized: there had to be a *bella ragazza* in the picture. I would quiz him on it when we were alone.

"What are the cops doing outside?" He walked the fish into the cooler.

I started to help Landon cut out cannoli dough with a margarita glass as a cookie cutter.

"Eve was attacked!" Landon said.

We filled him in on the events of the last two hours. It was very satisfying to see him scowl. When we were done, just after I threw in that Maria Pia had hired Belinda DiMaio but I was going to fire her because I had hired Joe Beck instead, he asked, "Do you think the theft has anything to do with the murder?"

"Like maybe Arlen was in cahoots with his killer?" Landon wrapped a cutout around the cannoli tube.

"I think it has to be related somehow," I told them, grabbing for a bowl for the filling, "but I don't know how."

Choo Choo grabbed a twelve-inch frying pan from the overhead rack and slammed it on to the front burner. Then he started pressing a knife handle on several cloves of garlic like he was trying to get them to give up a secret formula. Maybe because of his size, he had a domineering presence in the kitchen, a kind of Us/Them attitude — and They were all inanimate objects. Pots, pans, produce, pasta. You'd think it would make him clumsy, but not so. He was a wonderful cook. But every meal was a battle between pre-food and the forces of good.

Landon slipped in his CD of *Anything Goes,* and I took a quick break to dance a few bars of the fabulous Sutton Foster's routine from the Act I closing number while we all sang along. Then the Quaker Hills

PD crime scene unit showed up and spent about an hour in the dining room, mainly dusting the shadow boxes for prints, while my cousins and I got our setups and preps done for the evening's menu.

Since it was really warm outside and the wind was still, we figured on a big courtyard crowd, so Choo Choo went out the back to check on the tiki lights.

Then Dana showed up, hours before she was supposed to — wearing the exact same red sheath I had on. Hers did not look as though she had tussled with a puma. But on a day when I was making a decision to spoliate some hard evidence, defying my nonna on culinary matters, alienating my lawyer, and getting bagged and manhandled (without any of the really good stuff happening), I had used up all my available shock and dismay.

"Eve," she said, sounding like someone died and she was elected to tell me, "can we have a word? In private?"

"Sure, Dana," I said, wiping my hands on my apron and heading into the dining room. I pushed aside the table linens, topped with the two folded delivery bags, and sat down in the big booth. Dana settled into one of the chairs, completely oblivious to the duplicate dress imbroglio. "What's up, Dana?"

I had rested a still-floury hand on the table, and she closed her manicured one over it. So there we were, holding hands. Never let it be said that I saw no action in my hot red dress.

"Eve," she said with excitement, "I got the gig at Le Chien Rouge! I get to sing Piaf!"

Whose reputation, we can only hope, could withstand the soulful stylings of Dana Cahill.

"Well, well," was all I could manage.

But, like the dress, she didn't notice. She let go and sat back, looking like she was anticipating a turf war with the local don. "But darling Eloise" — okay, right there she lost me — "wants me two of the same nights I sing here, Eve, and oh, what are we going to do?" She waxed waxy about how difficult it gets when one's in such high demand, but she was sure we were all reasonable people willing to work out something that would best benefit her career before the recording contracts pour in.

Straight face, Angelotta, straight face.

And then it struck me: was Dana keeping a straight face whenever I talked to her about getting back into shape and resuming my Broadway career?

When she released my hand, I set it out of reach. Do I fire her outright? How could I do that to a friend?

As I formulated a response, I realized that something was bothering me about the dining room, but I couldn't put my finger on it. Had the thief taken something else, which I hadn't noticed yet?

"Well, Dana," I said, "I'm happy for your new gig" — she sat up straighter and brightened up — "but you're going to have to choose."

You would think I was speaking Uzbek. "Choose?" she said, all of her features collecting around her nose.

"Between Le Chien Rouge and Miracolo." Probably the only brilliant thing I had come up with so far that day.

"But why?" she sputtered.

Figuring it out as I went along, I said I believed she needed to be careful not to overexpose herself as a performer. I added an analogy about how people all love what's rare and turn their backs on what's common. And I finished up by assuring her that I'd understand perfectly if she chose Eloise Timmler's fine establishment.

And at that moment I realized I would miss her. I'd miss having her around because she's an affectionate person who truly loves what she does, even if she doesn't do it particularly well.

Puzzled at the idea of overexposure, but sensing it might not be good business, Dana said she'd have to think it over. But tonight she was ours. "Speaking of Eloise," she lowered her voice in her *Gossip Girls* voice, "I think she's got a guy."

I was scrutinizing the dining room, trying to pinpoint what was bugging me. So far, nothing. I sighed. "Oh, yeah?" Was it possible there was a man besotted enough to look past the health code violations?

"I just came from there — I figured I'd stop by during the slow time — and caught them in the kitchen." She went on to describe how cozy it had all looked, Eloise scraping off the grill, the guy running his hands around her waist. "Very cozy indeed. Pillow talk missing only the pillows" — Dana winked — "if you know what I mean."

Dana thought he looked kind of familiar, like maybe she's seen him around town. A cool kind of look, denim shirt, rugged looks. "And I said to myself, well, Eloise has got herself a Marlboro Man!"

Seriously? *Eloise Timmler?*

When Dana left to go work on her personal "choosing crisis," as she called it, I sat back in the booth and thought about the latest problem. What was the likelihood there was another Marlboro Man in town? It could happen, I supposed, drumming my fingers on the table. And my definition of this subspecies might very well differ from another's.

But I found myself feeling pretty narrow-eyed at the thought that Mark was up to something behind my back.

Or . . . was Mark up to something behind Eloise's back?

Either way, I didn't like it.

The front door swung open and Vera Tyndall appeared, early. While she handed me the linens delivery bags and started covering the tables, she talked about how much better her brother was doing and asked about Maria Pia. Pulling a Joe, I went all monosyllabic on the subject. Vera looked at me with a grin and kept working, her hair held back in a pretty black-and-gold headband. No one managed the Miracolo "look" better than Vera, who could somehow make you think that a white tailored shirt and black pants were a radical fashion statement.

Giancarlo arrived stiffly.

Followed by Alma, who had had bangs cut

— at the suggestion of her grief support group, she told me — and jazzed up her baggy black pants with a new sample of Art for Your Feet! Paulette breezed in, heard about the various crimes, and stacked the poor empty shadow boxes as though she was putting away kids' toys at the end of the day. When Jonathan sailed in with a basket of wine, I had a crazy moment of wanting to leave the Closed sign up and head out to the countryside with the staff for some late-afternoon wine and cheese alfresco.

I broke into all the chatter to tell them about tomorrow morning's meeting at Joe's for the Free Maria Pia operatives.

Choo Choo pushed through the double doors, and when Vera sailed a smile at him, I discovered my cousin's secret: he was sweet on Vera Tyndall. The ramped-up personal style, the small portions, the blush he was wearing that very second. My heart lifted.

I grabbed the two linens bags and went back to the kitchen, humming. Things suddenly didn't hurt so much — my shoulder, my pride, my grandmother, my uncertainties about Mark, my conversations with Joe, even the prospect of twenty years in the slammer. And, in honor of love, I decided

to make my special filling for the Great
Miracolo Cannoli Rebellion.

14

Four hours later I was in the middle of the dinner rush, up to my sleeves putting the finishing touches on an order of *scabeggio,* my favorite marinated fish dish, when I realized what I wanted to do: stake out Mark Metcalf. Garlic always sharpens my thinking. Content now, I reimmersed myself in the wine, garlic, lemon juice, and (user-friendly amounts of) sage aromas of my work.

When I stuck my head through the kitchen doors much later, Mrs. Crawford — resplendent in a butter-yellow full-length gown with black embroidery — was finishing up her last set with Miles Davis's "Kind of Blue." Vera was erasing the words *Ricolato cannoli* from the specials board, to the satisfying sounds of inconsolable anguish from the customers. And as the night came in through the front windows, I could half shut my eyes and let myself think our soft hanging globes and flickering table votives were moons and stars in some benign universe where the air was scented with lemon and garlic. A place where you could believe the men were honest and true, and the women could sing on-key. Is that too much to ask?

As the late-night regulars drifted in — including Dana, who had added a double strand of pearls — I watched the final two couples gather their bags and wraps. In the kitchen, Landon and Choo Choo were discussing the Phillies' chances.

I decided everything looked under control, which, of course, is always worrisome, but I kissed my cousins good night, saluted Li Wei, and donned a black zipped hoodie I yanked from the lost and found. With my black pants, black top (with hood fully deployed), and black Keds high-tops, I looked like a ninja homey. In terms of stakeout chic, it was a little too "in the box" for my taste, but as a newcomer I had to start somewhere.

As I slipped into the night, I got a grin from the smitten Choo Choo and a "Tell me you're going to a mime bar" from Landon. I snaked through what backyards I could between the restaurant and the north-east corner of Market Square, pushed my way through some uncooperative hedges, and emerged onto the side street that connected us to Callowhill Street, where the streetlights were so bright you'd think it was Madison Square Garden.

I dashed into the shadows, and tried on a hip-hop gait, head down, as I passed a group of college girls. I was jazzed. I was pumped. Clothes really do make the manic. When I was in range of Full of Crêpe, I oozed across Callowhill Street and looked totally suspicious loitering at the side of the Herb and Yarn Shoppe. On the one hand, I told myself, *Be bold,* and on the other hand, I thought, *What are you, nuts?*

Suddenly I wondered why it had not occurred to me to stake out Mark in my car. It would have made sense, parking across the street in an inconspicuous old car that draws about as much attention as a middle-aged lady in T-shirt and jeans in a bingo hall. But as Landon once pointed out to me, my brain always looks for the longest distance between two points. He calls it Eveometry.

When I hung back as a patrol car cruised down Callowhill Street, I realized Eloise's storage container in her driveway offered the perfect cover. Peeking around it, I could see that the restaurant was dark, but there were lights on in the back.

What's the plan, Angelotta? Well, first I should determine the worst-case scenario, which seemed to be discovery. Once I came to terms with that, I could relax and go for bold.

I decided to handle discovery by Mark with total honesty. The exchange would go something like this: when he asks what the hell I'm doing skulking around, I would go all Needy Mental Case on him, accusing him of cheating on me, making up a slew of broken promises he had never made in the first place, flinging our nonexistent fling at him. In short, full-out *pazza ragazza.* Crazy girl.

Most definitely a plan.

Of course, the stakeout might prove that Dana was hallucinating, and that Mark and I were just a matter of time. The office couch was going nowhere. So I actually tiptoed along the side of the pod and frog-walked my way past the crêperie windows. Although my thighs were screaming, my mouth was clamped shut. I rose upright just enough to get the lay of the land, stepped through the bushes lining the building, and cursed Eloise for planting something with stickers and prickers. What didn't scratch my ankles gripped me by my hoodie.

239

Then a loud metallic roar, pretty much like how I imagined the End of Days to sound, sent me sprawling on the ground between the bushes and the building. My heart was trying to burst out of my chest and the words *sitting duck* leaped to mind, but then I saw that the side floodlight was broken. *Phew.* I twisted a smidge to find the source of the noise.

Near the bottom of the driveway, the metal door of the pod had been rolled up and the storage unit was standing wide open. A dim Coleman lantern sat at the edge of the bay while a dark figure moved around inside, carrying something. It looked like a dead body, and my stomach lurched. What was in my karma that seemed to place me within twenty-five feet of corpses?

The Coleman lantern may have been helping the mysterious mover, but it wasn't clearing things up for me, clinging full of dread to the earth. But when I forced myself to take a closer look, I decided the shape of the Thing Moved looked more like a rug than a body.

Okay, so Eloise Timmler was still moving in. That was kind of boring. But then the window just above me slid open and a voice called out. I chewed the dirt.

"That you out here?" Eloise herself.

Presumably, she wasn't talking to me.

Indistinct mutterings from the pod.

"Come on in. I'll be done soon," Eloise said, and I heard her walk away from the window. When I heard two feet on the driveway I looked as far over my shoulder as I could, catching only the edges of the shadowy figure, who shut down the lantern, set it on the driveway, and pulled the pod's rolling door back down.

There was no way I could just leap up, push my way back through the bushes, and spring away into the night. So I stayed as motionless as I could and hoped for some deliverance that did not include being pulled upright by the hoodie.

Footsteps.

I swallowed hard.

When I caught a peripheral glimpse of the figure heading for the front door of Full of Crêpe, I shuddered with relief. Now would definitely be the time to ease myself to my feet and ooze off into the night, but I got stubborn. I wanted some answers.

After I counted to sixty, I rose up to the half-open window. Halfway across the dimly lighted room was Eloise Timmler spray-washing a pot. Lounging next to her was my Marlboro Man, Mark Metcalf. So Dana at least got that right: they knew each other.

Okay, so he was helping Eloise move in. Nice of him. This was one of the reasons I liked him. He was helpful, like an Eagle Scout. How he knew her, and for how long, and why exactly, were none of my business. (Which was both true and false all at the same time.) He'd probably just happened by Le Chien Rouge one day, craving something sweet and syrupy, and knew her as a customer. Maybe there was a little flirtation between them, whatever Dana saw or thought she saw, but was that any reason to —

They started talking, but it was hard to make out the words over the sound of the power spray hitting the metal pot.

Eloise: "— much longer, Mark."

Mark: "— patience, it's not —" (He stepped behind her and nuzzled her neck, and my mouth went grim.)

Eloise, who sprayed the wall by mistake: "— risk just keeps —"

Mark the Bum: "— beyond our wildest —" (He supplemented his clichés with some hand work that I, after three dates, had never seen.)

Eloise, who dropped the pot: "— last time, I don't think I —"

Mark the Groping Bum: "— baby, sweetie, tastykake —"

"Tastykake?" I mouthed. Was he kidding me? I didn't know about Eloise, but the word *tastykake* always put me in mind of round, chocolate-covered dream treats with a layer of peanut butter inside — not sex. But clearly, the crêpe cook and I were different people. She attracted Marlboro Men. I attracted corpses.

Since I didn't want to stick around to learn just what the word *tastykake* led to, I elbow-crawled and frog-walked my way back down the driveway to the cover of the pod, to steal silently into the night. But not before running into the Coleman lantern, which fell over with a clatter.

Saturday

As I hung out with a ratty afghan in my butterfly chair at 1 a.m., with a shot of Laphroaig in my hand, I took turns between pondering Big and Little Dippers and the faithlessness of men. In the partial moonlight the constellations were particularly lucid, which was more than I could say for myself. I sipped a little more. Looking up at the brilliant night sky was all I could do, because gazing toward the center of Quaker Hills was making me sadder than I could stand.

I knew that I was really kind of lucky to

be just a witness to Mark's faithlessness and not more intimately involved. When finally neither the afghan nor the Scotch kept off the night chill, I went back inside my tiny Tumbleweed home, locked up, and climbed alone up to my sleeping loft.

In the morning I woke up in a bad mood. So it didn't help that the milk was sour. And that I still couldn't figure out what was bugging me about the murder. And that I couldn't find my phone. And that I had a sudden craving for Tastykake. All this was bad, bad, bad. I threw on a top and a pair of shorts, and found my phone under the heap of stupid red dress I had kicked off the edge of the loft the night before.

When I headed out to my Volvo, even the dew on the grass bugged me. Some days it was galling that the world went on spinning, even when you were passed over by love and headed for twenty years in the slammer. If there was any spoliating to be done, I had wanted it to be by Mark. I was pretty sure that wouldn't have landed me in the big house. Hurling an epithet at the morning dew, I slammed myself into the car and realized there was some fog that could receive some choice words as well.

My GPS took me, bad attitude and all,

straight to Joe Beck's place for the meeting of the Free Maria Pia ops. It turned out to be a carriage house on the margin of the Quaker Hills Historic District, and I discovered that renovated carriage houses were right at the top of the list of what annoyed me that morning. It was old brick and old ivy and old slate roof. So trite. When I saw a silver Subaru that could only be his, I rolled my eyes. If he served anything other than Tastykake, I might blow sky-high.

Landon pulled up behind me, so I waited for him, scuffing my thonged toes in the gravel. He looked me over. I crossed my arms, adjusted my sunglasses, and crossed my arms again.

"Mime bar not work out?" he asked softly.

I looked around, then spilled it. "Mark Metcalf is seeing Eloise Timmler," I said through barely moving lips. "In a manner of speaking."

"Ah," said Landon. "And Mark Metcalf would be . . . ?"

"Well, this morning I'm thinking he's not the love of my life, after all."

Alma and Vera crunched across the gravel toward us. I gave them a wan smile.

Landon went for reasonable. "Perhaps he has an explanation that wouldn't rule out the love of your life part."

I snorted. "And Tastykakes grow on trees."

Kayla and Dana crunched across the gravel together. I shot 'em a world-weary look.

Landon grabbed my arm and steered me toward Joe's front door, which, lucky for Joe, did not have a cutesy sign reading Welcome Friends on it. "Suspend judgment," whispered my cousin.

I kept my sunglasses on and, when Joe let us in, muttered something that had some of the right syllables to be taken for "Good morning." With his jeans, he was wearing the kind of shirt that makes you think he likes the Great Outdoors. And he was barefoot. That morning I didn't care for feet. Or Crate and Barrel coffee cups. Or gravel. He had all three. He also had a few sisal rugs, saddle-brown leather couches, bookshelves with actual books, and a wall of windows at the back so he could look out at the fog and the gravel while he sipped French-press coffee from those Crate and Barrel coffee cups.

"Cara mia!" chirped Landon. "Your hair!" As he started raking his fingers through my hair, I realized that I hadn't combed it. I accepted the offered coffee, my sunglasses in place. Let everyone think I had tied one on last night, or woken up with a migraine.

Landon brought me a plate that held a toffee brioche, which I accepted wordlessly. A brioche on a plate is better than a Tastykake in the head.

Then I sat silently, shoulder to shoulder with Landon.

When Joe shot him a look like *What's wrong with her?* Landon gave him a face that said *Dunno, this is how I found her.* I elbowed him and he winced. Once we were all assembled — Choo Choo, Paulette, Jonathan, Alma, Kayla, Vera, Landon, Dana, Joe, and I — Joe made his report. He had visited his client, Maria Pia, in jail yesterday afternoon and discussed the evidence with her. (Here he looked at me and I could tell he was itching to ask about the bracelet, so I slid my sunglasses down just far enough to give him the look that usually precedes an especially vigorous *malocchio.*)

Undaunted, he went on to tell us that he'd explained that she'd be arraigned on Tuesday — which meant she'd hear the formal charges and enter a plea of Not Guilty — after which she'd be out on bail. He'd assured her that we were all at work on the investigation, and that the blue kimono Choo Choo had brought did indeed look lovely on her.

Suck-up, I thought with a smirk.

He looked directly at me. "Only because she asked."

Then he called for a report on any recent findings.

Alma reported that Sasha Breen of Airplane Hangers was having her hair colored at the time of the murder — which Alma had verified — and that she'd agreed to display three pairs of Toscano's Tootsies. We all clapped. Alma blushed.

Jonathan reported the results of his research on Mather. Dabbing his lips with a napkin, Jonathan told us about Mather's golf handicap, his charitable donations for the past year, and his attendance at three different interior design trade shows. I wondered what light any of this might shed on the murder, but Landon gushed and we all clapped anyway, because we liked Jonathan a lot, and he seemed pleased.

Vera reported on Arlen Mather's address, his delinquent taxes, and his political party.

Paulette pulled out a spiral notebook, put on purple drugstore readers, and made her report on the east quadrant shops. A stakeout of the blind bookstore owner yielded the info that he was cheating on his wife, but three different witnesses verified his alibi for the time of the murder. Repeated quizzing of the old lady who owned the card shop resulted in having to personally drive her to the ER, where Paulette was happy to report that she fully recovered. As for the Korean kid at the dry cleaner's, she ended up following him to a martial arts class, where she learned he's a second-degree black belt and decided to eliminate him from suspicion. "I mean, why would he have to use a mortar on his victim?"

"To divert suspicion?" Landon put forward.

Paulette waved it away. "Anyway, he was in his AP calculus class at the time of the murder. His teacher verified it, and we're going out for drinks next Wednesday." We cheered and Paulette snapped her reading glasses shut with a modestly pleased look.

Choo Choo reported on Maria Pia's life in jail. Sympathetic whimpering ensued.

Kayla reported on a mole problem at the farm.

Landon reported on the evidence against our nonna, just so we all knew what we were up against. Neither he, Joe, nor I mentioned the silver bracelet.

When my turn came, I sipped my triple-ethical (organic, shade grown, fairly traded) coffee and said cryptically that I was pursuing inquiries. This grave pronouncement was met with some nods and furtive looks.

So many furtive looks, in fact, that I found myself wondering what all *their* alibis were.

Then Dana, who had waited for all the other operatives to wind down, stood up, smoothed her skirt, and informed the rest of them that the dead Arlen Mather was actually a man named Max Scotti. She and Patrick had known him as a financial adviser. And apparently Mr. Scotti was an opera lover.

Everyone reeled with all this new information. Energy surged; coffee cups were refilled.

Alma stepped up and insisted on investigating the personal history of Maximiliano Scotti.

Jonathan teamed up with Landon to go door to door in the deceased's old neighborhood, wherever that may be.

"Mather's?" asked Vera. "Or Scotti's?"

Landon and Jonathan consulted briefly. "Mather's."

Vera said, "Then I'll take Scotti's." Since that could be harder to find, she asked Choo Choo if he'd like to team up with her.

We all took his speechlessness for assent, and he spent the rest of the meeting with a glazed look on his face.

Paulette assigned herself the task of investigating Mrs. Crawford, citing the old crime-solving adage, *Cherchez la femme.*

"Good luck with that," was all I said. When Joe laughed, I caught his eye — and his smile — and didn't mind the bare feet or the gravel so much.

"Also Li Wei," said Paulette, adding his name to her list.

Also Gian-car-lo Cres-pi, she scribbled.

Everyone seemed a little alarmed at her thoroughness.

"Vera," I said suddenly, turning to her, "you were the first to arrive yesterday." Now that Joe's fine caffeine was zooming through my system, I still couldn't shake the feeling that something was off yesterday in Miracolo.

Vera nodded, interested.

"Did anything seem odd to you, in the dining room?"

I had the attention of all the other ops.

Vera tipped her head. "Like what, Eve?"

I shrugged. "I just keep having the feeling that maybe something else got stolen in the robbery. Only, I haven't figured it out yet."

"Well . . ." She tried to reconstruct the scene, "I came in . . . I told you how much better my brother Eric's doing . . . we talked about Maria Pia . . . and I covered the tables with the clean linens." Which was pretty much how I remembered it, too. She opened her hands wide. "No, nothing struck me, Eve. Just that all the opera stuff was gone."

The others had gotten bored and moved to the table for more goodies, but I said, "Tell me again, Veers. Nice and slow. Don't leave anything out."

Step by step, she recounted how she had come through the front door, called out "Hi" to me where I sat at the back of the dining room, and set her jacket on a chair. She walked over to the empty shadow boxes, said a few things about what a shame, and so on — which I remembered, as well — but nothing struck her as otherwise out of place. Then she had come over to me, telling me about her brother, handing me the empty linens bags from the top of the pile, grabbing an armful of tablecloths. And while she had covered the tables — nothing missing, all cloths accounted for — we talked about Maria Pia.

Maybe it had something to do with that part of our conversation. Some little piece of information had almost triggered something, a memory, an observation, a —

At that moment Dana took center stage on Joe's largest rug and made an announcement. "There is no easy way to say this," she began oratorically. Chatter dried up and heads turned toward her, goodies stalled midair. "But I have decided to accept another position."

This drew some puzzled looks.

"You're leaving Patrick's office?" asked Paulette.

"No," Dana said patiently, "my presence there is indispensable to the operation, so I will always be the office manager." She clasped her hands just under her chin. "I will be singing almost nightly at Le Chien Rouge."

This announcement was met with a general outcry that could only be called tepid.

She turned to me, hands clasped like a supplicant. "Which means tonight will be my final performance at Miracolo."

Something akin to a huzzah went up, which Landon then explained to her meant we were all thrilled for her career advancement.

Totally our loss, said someone.

Eloise Timmler's gain, said I, remembering Mark's gropes.

Whatever will we do? (This from Paulette, who hid behind a napkin.)

Leo the mandolin regular will just have to soldier on.

Brett on the homemade bass will just have to man up.

Awash in our support, Dana practically

twirled, babbling about how she hoped we'd understand that these new demands on her time meant she could no longer participate in Operation Free Maria Pia, and that she hoped we'd stop by to hear her stylings of that little wren, Edith Piaf.

15

When the meeting broke up fifteen minutes later, Landon and I thanked Joe and headed for the door. "Oh, sure thing," he said casually, turning to say something to Alma. Not for a second did it look like he was going to peel me off my attentive cousin and harangue me about withholding evidence. With a sigh, I realized he had written me off. I only hoped it was because he was concentrating all his energies on Nonna's bail and eventual defense.

On the drive to Miracolo, I debated tonight's dinner specials with Landon. I settled on potato gnocchi and *maccheroni con la trippa,* a delicious sausage soup from the Piedmont area. Landon bickered with me a tad over the wisdom of making soup at the end of May, but I insisted we could crank up the air-conditioning. After all, it was intoxicatingly fragrant. And Maria Pia's dime paying the utilities. Landon relented.

We spent a lovely afternoon having a three-way gnocchi-making race, Landon, Choo Choo, and I. By the time we were done, we set aside our gnocchi boards and counted: Choo Choo, who had very agile thumbs for such a big guy — and the secret of making good, light gnocchi lies in the thumb — beat us by about fifteen gnocchi. Landon decided on two different aromatic sauces to pair with the gnocchi and got busy with tomatoes.

By the time we opened our doors, the waitstaff had arrived. And finally Mrs. Crawford, decked out in white silk pants and a navy silk tunic with a mandarin collar and powder-blue embroidered lotus flowers. Her wiry hair was swept up off her neck with a couple of chopsticks. Jonathan was back on duty as sommelier, which put a spring in his cute little step, and Choo Choo had changed into his maître d' outfit. I was strictly black pants, black chef jacket, and black toque.

We looked sharp.

We were sharp.

The first half of the evening went so smoothly, you'd think we had been professionally choreographed. Nothing boiled over, nothing broke, no double bookings, no drunks. At eight o'clock, I stepped back from the Vulcan range and took a few deep breaths. My *maccheroni con la trippa* was nearly gone, enough for maybe three more servings, but the wonderful smell of the succulent sausage remained like a delectable ghost.

I looked around. Li Wei was bopping along to his iPod, and Landon was plating two orders of the gnocchi. Life was good. I ambled over to the double doors and peered through the glass into the dining room, where Mrs. Crawford's chopsticks were failing, although her fingers were not. Only one empty table. It was very satisfying to hear the chatter, the pleasurable laughs, the soft jazz.

And then I noticed the group of four at table 7.

It was Joe Beck.

And James Beck.

And James's wife, Olivia.

And another woman. She was wearing a white silk blouse with a deep ruffled neckline and a black pencil skirt. The bling was gold. The hair was gold. She looked like someone who had grown up with money in a household where even the cupcakes were monogrammed.

She could have been a horseback-riding Bryn Mawr debutante, whose idea of slumming was spending summers on Martha's Vineyard with Mumsy and Daddy. But could she dance Sutton Foster's entire routine for the title song of *Anything Goes*? Could she make *maccheroni con la trippa* from scratch? Could she even pronounce it?

But I had to admit, she did kind of look like she went with Joe.

I heaved a sigh.

I could go right out there and meet her. After all, I'd paid a buck to hire Joe as my lawyer, so it might be okay to interrupt their split of champagne and thrust out a hand. She would lift her professionally waxed brows at me, and Joe would explain that I'm the head chef. Then she'd ask politely whether I had to go to school for that.

On second thought, I'd just stick to the kitchen.

I watched Joe make a toast, then James made what must have been a witty response, because all four of them laughed. When I realized that my nose was actually pressed against the window, I sprang back in horror. The Becks — "monied" folk, as Uncle Dom would have called them — lived in a world that would never include me. I was just someone who made food for them, in the back, out of sight. They would never see my face or even know my name. Sooner or later, even my "lawyer" would forget it.

A buck goes only so far.

The rest of the evening flew. I kept my head down when Li Wei broke a wineglass, and I kept my head farther down when I b——d the veal I was pan-frying and had to start the order over. Alma got a handsome tip from the Becks, then they left. When the dining room was empty, Mrs. Crawford evaporated. Fewer late-night regulars than usual turned up. Dana got through her swan song with a minimum of missed notes, then half cried a farewell and full-out pitched her new gig into the mic.

There is certainly nothing I like better than advertising another establishment.

Paulette, Vera, Jonathan, Choo Choo, and Alma all said good-bye and left.

The regulars packed it in earlier than usual, as did Giancarlo.

After Li Wei slipped out the back door, I told Landon — who knew something was up with me but was too tired to ask — to go. I'd finish up alone.

So what was I feeling, in a week when I'd been bagged and burgled; a week when I'd discovered a dead body right here in my kitchen, and my grandmother was carted off to jail and I decided to hide some evidence; a week when my life seemed to consist only of nights alone and days cooking?

We wait for our real lives to find us and begin — that's what I was feeling. Like those lives were offstage somewhere, waiting for us, while all the time we were here, waiting for them. And sometimes the lives we think we've left behind are really all around us. Like the stars and geraniums, and cousins you can count on.

I rummaged in an old canvas bag on the bottom of the office closet and pulled out a beautiful, beat-up pair of tap heels, slipped them on, and fastened the straps. Then I plugged the *Anything Goes* CD into the sound system, clicked through to the final number in Act I, the title song, and cranked it all the way up. And pushing the prep table to the far side of the kitchen, I danced. Flap heels, chugs, double- and triple-time steps, wings, paddle turns, and riffs — I danced, slamming my taps off the metal sides of the worktables and counters whenever I could. What I didn't remember of the choreography I made up, throwing in Maxi Fords and Cincinnatis wherever the music let me.

I tapped through all the men taken by others. I tapped through the sight of the murder. I tapped through the never-ending years of saltimbocca, no matter how good, that stretched out ahead of me; I tapped past the end of the music. And when I finally stopped, breathing hard, everything around me, the stove, the walk-in fridge, the prep table, and the pots and pans, all seemed to watch me in awe.

Because there I was. Not just a head chef who used to dance.

Still a dancer.

Sunday

Over a cup of espresso on my padded window seat (a couch wouldn't fit in my 130 square feet of living space), I looked outside. Some people leave boots out on their porch, some leave flip-flops, some leave garden clogs. Me, I left my tap shoes there when I got home at 1 a.m. Cradling my cup in my hands, I cataloged every aching muscle from last night's dance spree. To be fair, I think the shoulder was still the fault of my attacker.

Was I really considering leaving Nonna in a chefless lurch? I felt an unwelcome twinge of conscience. And did I think it would be a slam-dunk to get work in New York after three years? *Eve who?* When I started to sound too much like Scarlett O'Hara in my own head — *Where will I go? What will I do?*

261

— I set my empty cup in the sink and headed out to the Volvo.

There were certainly ways in which I didn't trust Maria Pia. For instance, I was convinced she had left out some key ingredients when she passed on a few of her own recipes, and let's not even touch the whole plot to get me out of town in order to redecorate Miracolo while I was gone. But I was certain that she had not killed Arlen/Max.

Maybe I was just stuck in that far kingdom of my own blindness, where I believed Mark Metcalf kind of liked me, where Dana would never dare to shove off from Miracolo's lazy, hazy shore, where no bad would come to me for hanging on to the silver bracelet Nonna dropped at the crime scene. But, bottom line, I knew Nonna was innocent, and I was going nowhere until Operation Free Maria Pia could spring her.

When I pulled up outside Miracolo, there they were, waiting: Alma, Paulette, Vera, Choo Choo, Landon, Jonathan. Dana was missing, treating us to our first awareness of her cutting off the old allegiances. She was probably off somewhere rehearsing a Piaf playlist. I felt strangely lonesome.

So I parked and then used my almighty new key to let the gang in to practice the tarantella for tomorrow's Festa della Repubblica dinner crowd. While they rehearsed, I'd inventory my supplies for the upcoming week.

As soon as the gang got inside, they started jabbering about sashes and dance partners and vests. From a canvas tote, Paulette produced six tambourines with streamers and passed them out. Everyone immediately started shaking and whapping them. Then, with a flourish and a whole lot of commentary, Landon drew out colorful sashes and black felt vests for the men. Everyone "oohed" at the sashes, which were the red, white, and green of the Italian flag, and Landon demonstrated on Jonathan how to tie the sash.

Then Vera dug into a backpack and pulled out three women's hair combs with long, colorful streamers attached, giving two to Alma and Paulette. Before long, Choo Choo, Landon, and Jonathan were fully outfitted in their black felt vests and colorful sashes, and Vera, Alma, and Paulette were wearing long white aprons and fussing at their hair decorations.

My job was to cue up the "Tarantella" CD.

Landon clapped his hands, and everybody paired off. Landon was teamed with Alma, Choo Choo with Paulette, and Jonathan with Vera. At Landon's cue, I turned up the volume. "Five, six, seven, eight!" called Landon and the three pairs started the tarantella step, a combination of light kicks and steps, followed by the tarantella do-si-do. Sashes swished, streamers bounced, tambourines went rogue. For a while I watched, sitting in a booth — the one where I'd been sitting on the day of the attack — while making out the next week's shopping list.

When the music ended, Landon cried, "People!" and launched into a lesson on tambourine skills.

I headed back to the storeroom to check on the supply of semolina flour and votive candles. The door softly shut behind me as I flicked on the light, and I had an uneasy moment when I remembered struggling to free myself from the double bags. This was my first time in the storeroom since it had happened. Except for the nervous tic that started over my right eye, I pronounced myself PTSD-free. *Flour, flour, flour.* On the shelves at the back I found pastry flour and bread flour, but we were going to need to get our hands on some prime semolina to get through next week's homemade pasta needs. How had I let the supply get so low?

Then I pushed aside the glass vases that

we hadn't used in a while — and my hand started shaking. *Okay, okay, eye tic, trembling hand. So you're a little more upset than you're letting on. It's no big deal. All's well that ends well,* I chuffed at myself, offering up the cut-rate wisdom you hear only from those who have never experienced anything, oh, untoward. Like, say, the blond beauty with Joe, a woman who's probably never been scolded, never failed — certainly never been bagged and dumped. Talk to me, blond beauty, when you fall off the stage at the New Amsterdam Theatre, or when your dad takes off when you're a teen, leaving behind a note that doesn't even mention you. Talk to me when you discover a corpse in your kitchen. Talk to me then.

By then my throat was tightening up as I stood, free and safe, in the well-lighted storeroom. Never mind the trembling hands or tics over the right eye and now below the left. I was fine and dandy. Anybody messes with me, I had cans of olives I could hurl. Biting my lip, I sank against the shelves holding the canned goods, the feeling of being strapped into the linens delivery bags rushing at me. The realization that I'd been hauled and dumped here like a sack of potatoes. The sound of the door slamming, a chair jammed up against it, trapping me inside. Then kicking and struggling against the bags and the sensation of being smothered, until I managed to rip my way free.

I swallowed hard.

Settle down. Settle down. It's over. Aside from the theft and a bruised shoulder, nothing terrible had happened. *Just leave. Get out of the storeroom.* But, aside from sliding down to the floor, I couldn't move. And I was pretty sure I was hyperventilating. I grabbed a small brown bag and started gasping into it. With my luck Joe would turn up right about now, finding me sweating and hacking into a paper bag.

At least when Mark the Groping Bum had freed me, I was standing on my own two feet. A woman of action. Dashing around, thrusting the bags at him, assessing the loss, calling the cops. He was nothing but a blur to me at that time.

Come to think of it — I stared at a spot on the floor while the little brown bag kept inflating in and out, in and out — what happened to the delivery bags? Tomorrow Arne the Austrian would be back to trade the old bags and tablecloths for new. What the heck had Mark done with them?

As if I weren't irritated enough with the man. As if I'd ever take him back, even in my fantasies, after watching him feel up the likes of Eloise.

I dropped the paper bag and scrambled to my feet, looking around. Where had he taken them off to? In all the confusion after I discovered the theft, the routine stuff flew out of my head. If I couldn't find the linens bags, would Arne charge us for the loss?

I checked behind the stacked canned goods and boxes of fluorescent lightbulbs. I checked in the big pile of dish towels. I checked behind the boxes of replacement glassware. Every corner of the storeroom I searched. I didn't find the bags, but my hands were steady now and I could at least breathe normally.

I strode back into the kitchen, glancing around. No bags. So I went back into the dining room, where the troops were still polishing their tambourine skills, and sat back in the booth where I had recovered from the attack, my arm resting on the pile of clean tablecloths that day. I called out, "Say, has anybody seen the linens bags Arne delivered the other day?"

Paulette was clearly scouring her memory banks.

Jonathan and Alma shook their heads.

Landon asked, "Have you checked the —"

"Storeroom?" I cut in. "Yes."

Choo Choo gave a mighty shrug. The

black vest didn't move.

But Vera said, "You had them, Eve."

Blow me down. "I did?" Then: "When?"

"When I came in for work. Remember?"

"No," I said slowly. What was she talking about? "What day?"

"The day it happened." She gestured to the walls. "The theft."

"No, I didn't," I said, confused. What was tickling at my brain?

Vera came toward me, pointing to the booth. "Sure you did. Right where you're sitting now." My head jerked to the right. The booth was empty, but a strange feeling started to sink through me. Whatever had been bugging me, whatever had been jiggling at my memory those past couple of days, was trying to surface.

"The tablecloths were next to you, right?" Vera asked.

I nodded slowly, trying to get the complete picture. My hand settled on the imaginary pile of table linens that Arne had delivered.

"Remember?" she asked. "I took them and started —"

"Covering the tables," I finished.

Vera nodded. "Well, the delivery bags were right on top."

"On top of the pile," I repeated, trying to envision it.

"Right."

How on earth did they get there?

Think. Get the picture.

I remembered dashing out of the store-room, pushing past Mark, thrusting the bags at him. Right there, in the doorway to the storeroom. But they weren't in there now, so he didn't set them down there. I was pretty sure I hadn't touched them after that. And none of the waitstaff had touched them. But they ended up on the pile of clean tablecloths. So while I was dashing around, checking out the wreckage of empty shadow boxes, Mark must have folded them and placed them on top of the pile.

But why?

Why there?

He must have done it automatically.

But *why* automatically?

Because . . . that's where he had found them.

As the truth rushed at me, I felt sand-bagged all over again. That's where Mark had found the bags, when he had slipped into Miracolo before he was due to meet me. When he found the perfect things to get me out of the way without really hurting me . . . while he stole all our opera memorabilia.

16

There's something doubly unsettling about discovering (a) you had something of real value when all along you thought it was cool but worthless stuff, and (b) someone has gone and stolen it. I was utterly baffled why Mark would go to such elaborate lengths to make off with my little personal treasures. I had never fooled myself that they had any real monetary value outside our walls. So why would Mark run such a risk?

While Landon took the tarantella dancers through their paces again, I slipped into the kitchen and poured myself a drink of water. Then I paced the kitchen floor, trying to think it all through. Had he set me up right from the start? What would that even mean?

I found myself standing right over the spot where Mather's body had been lying just five days ago. Dying over a Caruso 78.

Were Mark and Arlen Mather in cahoots? What if the 78s were the key, somehow?

But the key to *what*?

And why would they be in cahoots? Did they plot to rob us but then had a falling-out? I rolled my eyes. *Oh, right, Eve: cahoots, plots, falling out.* There was probably a perfectly reasonable explanation for why Arlen was found sprawled and dead over my record. Such as . . . ?

Such as . . . he wanted to try it in a different display. Such as . . . he wanted to sing along with Enrico. Or he wanted to take a picture of it to use in a lovey-dovey card he was making for Maria Pia. Or he wanted to pass it on to Mark Metcalf . . .

Or not.

Maybe he wanted to steal it before Mark could get wind of it.

Was the recording really so valuable?

Maybe the real question was whether it was worth killing for?

Okay, Eve, so apparently now you're saying Mark killed Arlen Mather. Isn't that a bit of a leap? No reason to assume he's more than a criminal-impulse shopper. And if Arlen had screwed him over somehow, and Mark had indeed beaned him to death, wouldn't he have made off with the Caruso 78? Unless somehow he thought taking the one thing from a shadow box that had any value would lead the cops to him. So maybe then

271

he'd leave it with the body and just bide his time, hoping he'd nab it in the end.

My brain was starting to hurt. I needed more information. A *lot* more information. Geoffrey Calladine was probably still asleep in Vancouver, so I'd have to wait on that one. In the meantime, what did I know for sure?

I was pretty sure Mark bagged and dumped me in the storeroom. The last time I ran into him on the street, I'd bragged about my opera stuff and set up the Friday meeting. At the restaurant, because he wanted to see me "at work." Right there, I should have known something was up. How many men go squishy over watching a woman at work? Unless, of course, she works at a strip club. So forget the idea of his being in cahoots with Arlen Mather. All Mark needed was me, alone, leaving the door unlocked for him. Bag me, dump me, help himself to the goodies.

As I stood musing, Landon came into the kitchen, the tarantella tune following him inside. "Eve," he whispered, "that guy is here."

I frowned. "What guy?"

"The cowboy guy. The one you had me check out for you that time." When I looked puzzled, he added: "Gay-wise."

Mark? *Mark* was here? "What did you tell him?" I grabbed him by the unitard.

Landon blinked at me in surprise. "That I'd see if you were busy."

Part of me really wanted Landon to tell Mark that I was nowhere to be found. But something had brought him here, and I wanted to know what. This was a great opportunity to get more information. And if he had come to play me, I was going to play him right back. Besides, Choo Choo was on hand as a bodyguard if necessary.

So I grabbed a hand towel, pretending to be drying my hands, busy, busy, and followed Landon into the dining room with a smile on my face.

And there he was.

And there came that pang just below my rib cage. *Really, Eve? This guy sacked and dumped you, and you still like the package?* He was dressed in boot-cut jeans over square-toed boots and a green plaid shirt with pearly snaps. Yee-ha.

"Hey," I said softly, walking right up close, like I still liked him.

"All right, people," Landon raised his voice over the music, "up to tempo, please, and — go!" As the three couples bounced into the choreography, I shot Mark a smile.

Mark creased his eyes at me. "Just thought

I'd check on you," he said in that low voice as wide as all Wyoming.

"You sweet man." I puckered my lips at him, swishing the dish towel between us. "I'm fine." I snapped the towel, which made him grin and take half a step back. Then I looked him up and down and asked kind of provocatively, "How are you?" The way I said it you'd think I was asking for sex credentials.

The eyes got narrower, the smile wider, and the double meanings started flying around the room. "Good," he whispered, staring at my lips. "Real good."

What a jackass.

"But I have to tell you," I said, "I feel really bad about our missed . . . date."

"Mm-hmm."

He was giving nothing away.

"You wanted to watch me work," I said with a secretive smile. I let my eyes rove dreamily over his face and lowered my voice, hitching a finger in his belt loop. He took a manly step forward. "If that's what you want to call it," I teased, drawing on every seduction cliché I knew.

I had rendered him inarticulate. Teach *him* to steal the ruff of Ruffo.

"What do you say we reschedule?" I stepped up so close I could practically polish his pearly snaps with my boobs. "Say, tonight?" The bait.

He didn't back away. "Mmm," he murmured, "can't tonight — going to a show — but tomorrow night we could . . . get together."

I took a deep breath, making sure he heard it. "How can I wait?" I asked plaintively, making a little anticipatory noise.

He planted a soft kiss on my cheek, then took off with that semiswagger I used to find appealing.

I swung back to the tarantella dancers and the real world, thinking about the take-away.

He probably believed that I wasn't wise to him, was still hot for him, and was dim, dim, dim. No worries about me. And I had learned that tonight he had plans. *Going to a show.* A perfect opportunity, I thought with a grin. For what, I didn't know. But at least it was a start.

Then I did something I had done only three other times since I had ascended to the head chef throne: I put Landon in charge. Head Chef for a Day. He promptly promoted Choo Choo to sous chef (Vera clapped her hands) and Jonathan to maître d'. Since Jonathan didn't have a suit, Landon left with him for Philly to find one before it was time to start prepping.

I did a quick check-in on the other "ops" to see how they were coming with their new assignments. Vera hadn't had a chance yet to identify Max Scotti's neighborhood and ring doorbells. Choo Choo reported that a phone call to Nonna yielded a stream of invective ("she cussed me out") about the recent dessert special, so in his opinion the Great Cannoli Rebellion had given her a reason to live. (Although he questioned whether, when she gets out, I can say the same.)

Alma reported that Maximiliano Scotti had an unblemished record as a financial adviser and that a seminar he had run on retirement planning had yielded two pages of glowing testimonials. She was still digging.

Then Paulette, collecting the tambourines, reported that her investigation had brought to light the facts that Li Wei Lin is here on an expired visa, Mrs. Crawford attends Gamblers Anonymous meetings in neighboring New Hope, and Giancarlo Crespi is generally thought to be an alias for the fugitive "Niccolo" from the Weather Underground who participated in bombings during the mid-'70s. While we all stood there with our mouths open, Paulette stuffed the tambourines back into the bag and said kind of absently that she was still digging.

"Well," I broke the stunned silence, "thanks, Paulette, for that update, and" — I riveted Alma, Choo Choo, and Vera with a look — "I don't have to tell you how critical it is to keep it all secret while the investigation is still ongoing."

Choo Choo looked like he was already longing for that simpler time, just five minutes ago, when our kindly arthritic bartender was just our kindly arthritic bartender. Alma and Vera moved closer together in a show of some sort of solidarity, which set Alma's Toscano's Tootsies jingling.

I desperately didn't want to know any of those things about anyone in our little Miracolo family, and part of me wanted to shake Paulette silly for destroying the pasta-making utopia that existed in my head. The woman's talents were totally wasted in rattling off the daily specials to a bunch of hungry customers.

"Whew," Vera said, fanning herself with her hand.

I made a short little speech about respecting others' private personal histories. But what if Paulette's discoveries actually had some bearing on the murder? Could Arlen

Mather have been blackmailing one of the three? Somehow I couldn't imagine that Mrs. Crawford would kill a man to keep from having her gambling problem from coming to light. It just wasn't the stuff of homicide.

But what about little Li Wei? How much did he have at stake? Was deportation enough to kill for if Arlen had found out about the expired visa? Maybe.

And then there was Giancarlo, our bartender for years and years. If he was on the lam from the feds for a set of old criminal charges, then it wasn't an insane leap to think that, if recognized, he might be driven to murder.

There was just no way I could make this line of reasoning come out all right. As the others all left, I decided to go on the happy assumption that Paulette was simply wrong. It was some other Giancarlo Crespi she had dug up. Made perfectly good sense. Such a common name.

Did I even need to run any of these revelations by my lawyer, Joe Beck? Or was I just adding to the pile of Things to Hand Over to Detective Ted that might result in Joe's throwing in the towel and leaving me lawyerless?

Risky, either way.

■ ■ ■ ■

"Calladine," came the cool voice at the other end.

"Eve Angelotta, Mr. Calladine."

"Oh, yes," he said slowly, "you had called about a Harlan Markman . . ."

"Right," I said. Then: "New day, new name, if that's okay with you."

The expert on classic opera recordings said, "All righty," and waited.

"Do you remember doing business with a Max Scotti?"

"Max? Of course! How *is* the old chuffer?"

I might not know what a chuffer is, but I could certainly answer the question. "Well," I said somberly, "I'm sorry to have to be the bearer of bad news, but Mr. Scotti died earlier this week."

Calladine took it surprisingly well. "What about his collection?" he inquired.

I assured him these were early days yet — "To be sure, to be sure," he said, probably to persuade me that he wasn't just a predatory clod — but that I'd be sure to let him know what was available after the estate settled.

"Tell me," he said with some energy, "did he ever get the Caruso?"

279

If I were a bird dog, I'd be quivering at attention.

"I spoke with Max just a few weeks ago, and he said he had a lead on one of the few extant recordings of Caruso singing 'Your Eyes Have Told Me What I Did Not Know' in English."

My heart leaped. "Did he now?"

"Oh, yes." Calladine laughed shortly. "Apparently he had come across it in the collection of an elderly friend . . ."

Nonna would positively self-combust, right after hurling a stupendous malocchio *at him, never mind that he was defunct.*

". . . but he had high hopes of getting her to make him a present of it."

So Max wouldn't have stooped to mere thievery. Maybe he figured he'd downplay the value of the recording and maneuver Nonna into giving it to him as a love token. *Steady, Eve.* I told Calladine I could say with certainty that the Caruso 78 was *not* in the collection of Max Scotti, but that I'd be sure to let him know if anything of Max's was about to hit the market.

By the time we hung up, I think we were both sparkling with pleasure. I had figured out just about as much as I was going to about the mystery of Arlen and our Caruso recording. But my mind still hovered around the likelihood that the killer had no interest in the 78 — otherwise he would have snatched it. Unless he had somehow over-looked it in the murderous heat of the moment.

I spent part of the afternoon at the public library at a computer, googling Li Wei, Giancarlo, and Mrs. C., without much success. Then I took to the Volvo and drove all around the commercial district of Quaker Hills, never pulling over, never stopping, like some kind of shark on wheels. *Keep moving or die.* To the casual eye, the driver of the Volvo was a Rastafarian — I had donned a dreadlocks wig attached to a crocheted hat in the colors of the Jamaican flag, which I had worn to a costume party in SoHo four years ago. To this ensemble I added a pair of John Lennon sunglasses.

Dana really did the disguise thing better, since the First Rule of Effective Disguise must be not to draw attention to oneself. But at least I had the cover of the Volvo. Outside my little work circle, I doubted my car was very recognizable.

As I oozed up and down the streets, the plan was just to reconnoiter. See who was around, and what they did. I'd stumbled upon Dana's photo shoot earlier; maybe now I'd stumble on something else that would crack the case wide open.

I drove, not too slow, not too fast. Turning corner after corner, easing to a stop at the lights, snacking discreetly on pico de gallo chips.

I saw Dana walking through Providence Park, in a midnight-blue dress, her black hair bouncing, heading toward Callowhill Street. My guess: on her way for her first day of work at Full of Crêpe. I stepped on the gas.

I saw Akahana getting into it with the trash collector, who had beaten her to the can outside Sprouts. I saw Patrick Cahill, in a pussycat-gray summer jacket, make his jaunty way over to Starbucks. Paulette exploded out of the dry cleaner's with a load of clothing on hangers, heading for the municipal parking lot. Adrian, the bouncer at Jolly's, came out of the Logan Building, where I guessed he was patronizing Massage Mania.

And then I caught sight of Mark Metcalf. He appeared to be window-shopping at Quaker Hills's only jeweler's shop, a funky store owned by Arnold Blitzen, called Blitzen Glitz. But it was already past five, and the shop was closed. Then Mark slipped his hands into his jeans pockets and headed up the north side of Market Square, right toward me.

I adjusted my shades and pulled my hat and wig combo farther down over my face, slumping at the wheel. When we passed each other and he didn't notice me, I moved forward and rounded the northwest corner of Market Square. I figured I'd go around the block and pick him up again on Callowhill Street, which is exactly what happened.

He stood waiting to cross the street ahead of me, and I flipped down the visor for a little more coverage. As I headed toward him, the idea of just gunning it crossed my mind. The creep.

I slowed at the yellow light; he raised a hand toward me in thanks; then he jogged to the far side of Callowhill Street. In my rearview mirror I saw him disappear behind Eloise's storage pod, so I pulled into a parking space and slunk down. Let the reconnoitering begin . . .

I watched customers enter the front door of Eloise's place, but didn't see Mark go in. The pod blocked my view of the driveway, and cars passed by in both directions. Then a wailing EMS truck. Then a school bus. So he might have gone in through the back and I missed him. Then another possibility occurred to me: maybe he let himself into the pod. When were the two of them ever going to finish moving her crap in?

Come to think of it, where was Eloise living? The building seemed to be only a story and a half high, with the upper windows boarded up and painted over with decorative designs. It looked like an attic, not an apartment. So where was all of Eloise's stuff getting hauled to? And why was the pod here, and not wherever she lived?

It felt weird to me.

But then, I was comfortable working side by side with fugitive bombers, and cannoli was my idea of revenge . . . Was I a good judge of weird?

At that moment Mark reappeared from the back of the pod, empty-handed. He wasn't carrying a box of books or an occasional table, for a home; and he wasn't carrying a commercial mixer or crate of glassware, for a restaurant business. He walked up to Full of Crêpe, and when he swung open the red screen door, a slightly off-key "La Vie en Rose" wafted outside.

Mark disappeared inside.

I just *had* to get into the pod.

But it would have to wait until after dark, when Mark was off at a show. With any luck, he'd take Eloise with him. By my calculations, 9:30 p.m. would be the ideal time for a return visit: after Full of Crêpe closed and before the theater let out.

How can I wait?

By 9 p.m. I was in range. I was back in my ninja homey outfit, the hood tightened around my face, some kohl from my theater days smeared over my cheeks. Even my shoelaces were black. I was a suburban commando — and my mission? Figure out what Mark was up to. If I could also rescue the ruff of Ruffo, so much the better. I parked in a dark stretch of DeWitt Street, two blocks off Market Square, one street north of Callowhill. I shut the car door as quietly as possible behind me, but a dog started barking in what I hoped was a fenced-in backyard. Some kindly homeowner yelled "Shut up!" which the dog seemed to take as encouragement.

I scrolled down the contact list on my phone and hit the button for Joe Beck. The Big Plan was fully formed, but I knew I'd need a smidge of assistance.

"Hello? Eve, is that you?"

"It is," I said in a low voice, hoping no neighbor would choose that particular moment to wheel his trash can to the curb. Darting into the protective cover of a box hedge, I went on. "I'm parked on the street behind Le Chien Rouge and I'm going to break into the pod in their driveway —"

"You're *what*?" he hollered.

Just then, the front door of a little Cape Cod bungalow next to my hedge opened. "Hang on," I hissed into the phone.

An old lady in a floral housecoat stepped outside, her hair looking like a puffball of cotton candy under the porch light. "Bootsie!" She made those hissy-kissy noises cat owners think entice kitties. "Bootsie!" When the prowling Bootsie did not appear, the old lady clucked her tongue and went back inside.

"Eve! Eve!"

I put the phone right up to my ear. "So here's how I see it," I said, squinting past the backyards on Callowhill Street, zeroing in on the crêperie. Happily, it looked dark except for a security light somewhere on the first floor. "Either you can come and help me out, which I figure increases my chance of success, or you can just show up at the police station when I fail miserably and explain to them how you knew about it beforehand and did nothing to stop it."

Dead silence.

I tiptoed along the side of the old lady's house.

"Tell me you're kidding."

"Mark Metcalf was the one who attacked me and stole my stuff," I informed him, just wanting to get on with it.

"Metcalf? Wait. Where have I heard that name?"

Oops, dangerous waters. "Oh, just a —"

But Joe was too fast. "Don't tell me he's the day trader you had your eye on."

"That's not the point," I said with dignity. I had to listen to Joe laugh out loud.

"Do you want to hear how I know, or not?" said I, bristling.

Joe could hardly keep it together. "So this paragon of manly virtue —"

"All right, all right, so I made a —"

"— bagged you," he blared into the phone. "Literally. Probably not quite what you had in mind — you in your pretty red dress. Talk about a hot date gone bad." When he stopped laughing, he asked, "Don't tell me you had your eye on the office couch?"

"It was good enough for the likes of you," I snapped.

"And you, apparently." Then he got mock-pensive. "I'm wondering what Freud would say about your needing to use the same place that Kayla and I —"

I topped him. "Freud would say *you* have intimacy issues."

"Unlike you, I at least have intimacies

before I have issues!"

I snorted. "If that's what you want to call
—"

But he overrode me. "You could have
taken your favorite felon back to your teeny
tiny little house."

I gasped. "How do you know where I
live?"

"I've driven by," he said casually.

I was furious. "Are you stalking me?"

"Oh, you'd like that, wouldn't you? You're
my client. I was bored, so I drove by just to
get the big picture."

I haven't put up with Maria Pia for thirty-
two years without having a state-of-the-art
Crap Detector. "Oh, right. Tell me another
one, Beck. You're just sad and blue that you
ended up with the wrong Angelotta on the
office couch." Yikes, where did that come
from?

It was his turn to gasp. "And you're just
mad you ended up with someone who was
more interested in what was on your walls
than in what was on your couch."

I was so angry, I could barely see the fence
I was going to have to climb to get into Le
Chien Rouge's backyard. "You've got fifteen
minutes, Beck. And," I added in a fake-nice
voice, "if you're coming, I suggest pocket
flashlights. And a set of lockpicks." Then I

hung up, turned off the phone, and jammed it into the pocket of my black hoodie.

17

With a grunt, I scrambled up and over the basket-weave fence separating the properties, then dropped six feet to the ground. I wish I could say noiselessly, but I discovered Bootsie the hard way. After the cat and I sorted out our respective panics, we split, and I skulked quickly to the back of the crêperie. If I jumped up and down, I could just see into the wall of kitchen windows. Empty.

To be sure, I spent the next ten minutes circling the building, peering in any windows I could reach. No easy chairs holding a snoozing Eloise. No signs of spontaneous floor passion featuring Mark and Eloise. From what I could tell, it was empty.

I moved to the pod and was examining the metal sliding door when a hand clamped across my mouth and an arm tightly encircled my waist.

"Hi, Joe," I said through his fingers as he pulled me out of the wash of the streetlight.

I managed to press the Indiglo button on my watch. Very good; he had arrived in thirteen minutes.

"Let's talk this over, shall we?" he whispered, grunting as he tried to wrestle me over to the grass.

"Look," I said reasonably as I tried to elbow him, "I haven't had a lot of experience with lawyers, but are they all so passive?"

"Passive?" he choked out as I struggled. His grip tightened. He was not helping the mission. "I haven't had a lot of experience with tap-dancing chefs," he hissed, pulling me off my feet, "but already I don't like them." As he stepped backward, he stumbled and we fell into a low azalea bush, cracking through branches as we went down.

"Now see what you've done," I said, wincing.

"What *I've* done!" In the dark, his eyes were flashing.

I pushed him away. "You haven't even heard my case." Since he seemed inclined to shut up and sprawl in the bushes, I laid it all out for him.

When I got to the part about how Mark Metcalf's theft of my opera stuff made me wonder about a connection to the murder of Arlen/Max, who was an opera memorabilia fan and found dead on my Caruso 78, Joe sat up, resting his arms over his knees. He appeared to be thinking things over.

"So I want to know what Mark's up to. I want to know why he took all my stuff, and where it is, and whether" — I gulped, because to tell the truth, I scared myself — "he had something to do with Arlen Mather's death." Even though the night air was warm, I shivered.

Joe was quiet for a minute. "How do you know it's safe to look around now?"

"He said he was going to a show tonight. I called the two playhouses in town, and their shows let out around eleven."

Joe finally reached into his back pocket and pulled out two mini flashlights, handing me one. "Keep the light off until we're inside the pod," he said softly, glancing quickly around at the neighboring houses. "And whatever we find inside, we leave it all there. We get the hell out and call the cops."

"But what about my —"

Joe grabbed my shoulders. "We get the hell out of there and call the cops. Anonymously." He heaved a sigh. "This has to be no-trace camping, Eve, otherwise I'll be washing dishes at Miracolo. If I'm lucky."

"Who needs lights when we've got you in a white shirt?" Though it looked slightly the worse for tumbling through the bushes and hitting the ground.

He shot me a look as he got up, digging around in his other back pocket. "Most of my breaking and entering experience" — he said through gritted teeth, pulling out a couple of small objects — "has been during daylight hours, so forgive me if I fail the dress code."

I stood and readjusted my ninja wear, tightening down the hoodie and smearing the kohl farther across my cheeks, and followed him over to the pod.

At that moment, two things happened. A patrol car started to come down Callowhill Street. Joe and I gave each other a look of horror and flattened ourselves against the metal door. And coming down the sidewalk from the other direction was a middle-aged couple. Ordinarily not a big deal, until we heard their conversation.

"Do you think they're open, Don?"

"I sure hope so. I'm really in the mood for her chocolate chip crêpes."

From what I could make out, the two of them were cutting across the yard toward the front door. And then we saw them. Any second now they'd give up on the crêpes, turn around, and catch Joe and me slammed against the metal door. And no part of that looked innocent.

I felt so panicked I could hardly breathe. If we slipped around the far side of the pod, we'd fall right into the high beams of the patrol car.

"Looks closed, hon," said the woman.

The guy swore. "Okay, let's go."

As they started to turn our way, Joe grabbed me, pushed the hood off my head and pulled me into a clinch, then kissed me hard, up against the metal door. One of his arms was wrapped around my hair, and the other held me so tight around my waist that I couldn't catch a breath — at least I think that's why I couldn't catch a breath — and I thought we'd sink right into the pod without even having to pick the lock.

"Oh!" said the woman, getting a load of us.

Although my eyes were flickering shut in the heat of the kiss, Joe's were steely, figuring out the next move. While the disappointed crêpe eaters muttered to each other about public displays of affection and started to move off, Joe's hand lingered at the small of my back, and I found myself thinking just how nice bruised lips can be, not to mention a nice bottle of Barbaresco and the sand on Key West.

The voices disappeared and Joe pulled slightly away, resting his fists on the metal door on either side of my head. The couple was gone, and the patrol car had passed the crêperie and continued on its way down Callowhill Street.

"Wow," I said, then, needing to explain further, added, "quick thinking."

"Sorry," he whispered, then turned toward the lock.

Should I tell him he now had kohl smeared on his cheeks?

But then I got interested in what he was doing with a ballpoint pen. He broke off the metal clip from the cap and bent the tip slightly. Then he handed it to me and set to work on a paper clip, which he straightened out, and then angled the tip.

"Hold the lock for me, Eve," he whispered.

When I cradled it in my hand, he turned it so that the large end of the key insert was on top.

While Joe slipped the bent tip of the pen cap into the key insert, I felt his breath on my hand. The thumb of his left hand lifted it up a little. Then he inserted the bent end of the paper clip just under the pen cap, as far as it would go.

"Here goes nothing," Joe mumbled, applying pressure to the pen cap as he wiggled the paper clip up and down.

The padlock fell open in my hand.

My eyes went wide.

With a quick look at the silent neighborhood, I slipped the lock into my pocket as Joe slowly raised the door just high enough to half crawl inside. We ducked into the mobile storage unit, and my heart started to flutter when Joe very slowly drew the metal door back down, plunging us into total darkness. When I was sure no one outside could see it, I flicked on the minilight Joe had given me.

Joe flicked on his own light and flashed it around, then whistled. The pod didn't hold leftover junk. He pushed past a couple of stacked crates marked Cherry Hill, and shined his light on two medium-sized rolled Oriental rugs leaning against the wall. If these were Eloise's, why hadn't they moved them into wherever she was living?

Joe's fingers cupped a tag fastened to one of the rugs, which he read and then glanced at me. "These are from the rug store two blocks away." He looked grim.

I swung my little light around, settling on a plastic bin holding a couple of Madame Alexander dolls, silver candlesticks, and Victorian jewelry. "This is Fran Beller's stuff that was stolen!" Looking into another small bin, I opened some newspaper wrapping and held up what I was pretty sure was the Baccarat vase from Frantiques.

"Look at this," Joe whispered from behind an armoire at the back. Dodging bins and crates, I made my way over. Crouched over a box, he held up what looked like some vintage clothing. Then I saw that it was Rosa Ponselle's corset, and Titta Ruffo's ruff! I bit off a cry.

"Is the demo record there?"

"Yeah. It's fine." He made a sweep with his arm. "This holds all the stolen property from Quaker Hills for the last three months. Your boyfriend's a one-man crime spree."

"Unless Eloise is in on it. And he's not my boyfriend."

Joe touched my arm. "Let's get the hell out of here and call the cops."

Then we both heard voices. Outside.

We flicked off our minilights.

"It's them!" I whispered. I had never felt so terrified.

He tensely whispered, "I thought the show didn't let out until eleven!"

What had Mark said? What had he *said*? *Going to a show.* "What if . . . he meant a movie, not a stage play. An early movie?" I felt myself sag.

The voices came closer. They were standing right on the other side of the door, and the two of them, Mark and Eloise, were arguing about the pod. *Where is the lock? Did you forget to put it on? Why do you always assume —*

"Go hide behind the armoire at the back," Joe whispered.

I sandwiched myself between the armoire and boxes stacked four rows high. In the total darkness I couldn't find Joe, and had never felt so alone and exposed. My skin crawled with the thought of what Mark might do to us if he found us.

The next moment I heard hands grip the handle and start to raise the metal door, which was the only thing that stood between us and calamity. Peeking out from my hiding place, I saw Mark's boots and jeans in the faint glow of the streetlights. I was petrified. The metal door scraped noisily up its tracks as Mark heaved it higher, and I saw Eloise turn and start up the driveway. The door was all the way open now, and Mark blocked the only way out.

Just as he stepped into the pod, holding the Coleman lantern, Joe sprang out from behind the tall crates.

"Hey!" Mark cried, dropping the lantern.

Joe whipped back his right arm and

dropped Mark with a single punch to the face.

As Joe stood over him he yelled at me to call the police, but just then I noticed Eloise. She took two shocked steps toward her fallen beau, then thought better of it and set off at a run. I dashed past Joe and the unconscious Mark and chased Eloise across half a dozen front yards, getting closer and closer. With a final effort, I surged forward and launched a flying tackle.

She went down with a thud, the wind knocked out of her. I was so blanked by the night's strange mix of kisses and loot and abject terror that as I held her down with a knee, all I could think to scream was, "No open garbage cans in the kitchen!"

Detective Sally turned up with a uniformed cop a few minutes later. While the cop handcuffed Eloise and loaded her into the patrol car, Sally took charge of Mark and the pod, calling for backup. By this time doors were popping open all along Callowhill Street, and curious neighbors stood in the glow of their porch lights.

Joe came over to where I sat, trembling, on the front lawn of someone who had offered me some iced tea. I had accepted it, then started crying

Joe slipped an arm around me without saying a thing.

"That was some punch," I managed finally.

"That was some tackle."

"Thanks." Then I got practical. "What did you tell Sally?"

Joe grinned. "I was vague. And she was glad I was vague. Oh," he added, "you might want to disappear the padlock." My hand flew to the bulging pocket of my pants.

While another patrol car, lights flashing, stopped nose to nose with the one holding Eloise, Joe went on to tell me that Sally and Ted were going to look into Metcalf's background and see if they could connect him either to Arlen Mather or Max Scotti. I shivered. How could I have been so completely wrong about somebody?

Another uniformed cop strode past us to the pod, his radio crackling.

"You okay?" said Joe, his gaze roving my face.

I nodded. "When can I get my opera memorabilia back?"

"Not for a few days. She'll make it as fast as she can."

I noticed two distant figures running toward us from the street connecting Callowhill to Market Square.

300

Just then, the cops walked the handcuffed Mark Metcalf past us to the waiting patrol car. Nose broken and bloody, groggy and stumbling like he was hungover, he looked like some small-time slime who had gotten caught. He didn't even look my way.

I scrambled to my feet. "Why my stuff?" I yelled after him angrily. "Why would anyone want Rosa Ponselle's corset?"

Mark half turned his bruised face toward me. "The money's in the demo record," he slurred. "The other crap?" He shrugged. "Habit." And the cops shoved him into the police cruiser, where he was pummeled by Eloise.

The two runners were now heading straight for us, and I squinted at them. It was Landon and Choo Choo, still in their chef jackets, their feet slapping hard on the sidewalk. *"Cara!"* they shouted.

I let out a cry. In that moment all I wanted was the safety of my passionate family, and I ran toward them, forgetting all about Joe.

Aside from some scratches and aches, I was doing pretty well. Still, once they got me back to Miracolo, I let Landon pull some fresh clothes for me out of the office closet and the Lost and Found, while Choo Choo set down a shot of Laphroaig. Part of me really wanted the attention, I won't lie.

Landon likes to think of himself as a calming presence, but as he flung garments at me over the Oriental screen in the corner, Bootsie the cat's histrionics when I landed on her tail had nothing on his. His hysterics are just a measure of his love, though, so I accepted the three-quarter-length siver-and-gold kimono, black spandex bike shorts, and low leopard-print boots. Then he handed me a warm, wet cloth to clean the kohl off my face in between slow sips of the peaty Scotch. Sunday night we close early, so by 10:30 the staff was trailing out into the night. Paulette had declared that I needed my sleep and they'd hear all about it tomorrow, so I set out for the Volvo dressed like a crazy person.

On the way home, I tried to take my lawyer's advice about disappearing the pod's padlock so no suspicion could fall to us. I even slowed the car as I crossed a brook, and slowed it even more as I passed a couple of empty lots. But I couldn't bring myself to toss the lock out the window. In a crazy way, it was a trophy from the night's adventures. I'd drop it in the Dumpster behind the hardware store tomorrow.

Monday

By the following afternoon, the news was definitely mixed.

Choo Choo reported that Maria Pia was languishing.

Alma Toscano reported that Airplane Hangers had sold two pairs of Toscano's Tootsies.

Ted reported that Mark Metcalf — whose real name was Shlomo Gertz — had a police record, and that they liked him for a string of thefts in southern New Jersey.

Shlomo Gertz?

Paulette reported that Li Wei's visa status was actually okay (we all cheered), but that the jury was still out on That Other Matter. With that, she eyed Giancarlo, who was polishing a martini shaker.

Sally reported that they could ascertain no prior connection between Shlomo Gertz and either Arlen Mather or Max Scotti. Good news for Gertz, but bad news for the murder investigation.

Dana reported with alarm that Le Chien Rouge was closed indefinitely, and could she pretty please have her job back? By way of persuasion, Patrick Cahill sent flowers, delivered to me personally by James Beck. All totally unnecessary, because I told Dana with a big smooch that Miracolo had missed her — okay, *I* had missed her — then we stood around for a while with our arms over each other's shoulders.

Landon reported with barely contained glee that (a) he was prepared to demonstrate how to make homemade pasta today for early patrons as part of Miracolo's Festa, and that (b) yesterday's suit shopping had determined that Jonathan's shoulders were even broader than one would think. This second point he delivered to me privately.

Ted reported that Shlomo had an unassailable alibi for the time of the murder: a root canal in the Logan Building, which took particularly long because he was being a baby about the shots.

We all agreed that there went the number one suspect in the Mather murder, which meant the killer was still at large.

Mrs. Crawford — resplendent in green and white tulle, complete with red snood, all for Italy — sat composed and inscrutable, taking it all in.

I reported that *calamari con pomodoro* was the entrée special on Festa della Repubblica, because today we were upgrading Tuscany to Honorary Northern Italy, and that Landon Angelotta was being promoted temporarily from sous chef. Gasps and cheers ensued.

Joe Beck made no report, because he wasn't there. Where's a good lawyer when you really need one?

A bit behind the clock, Landon and I were speed-slicing the tomatoes for the *pomodoro* sauce when Choo Choo stepped into the kitchen. "Vera found this in the foyer," he explained, handing me a pale violet envelope addressed to Eve Angelotta. "It was slipped under the front door."

I wiped my hands on my apron as Choo Choo returned to the dining room. Landon cranked up the original Broadway cast recording of *Wicked* while I sliced open the envelope.

The front of the card featured some colorful, stylized pansies. Inside was a note in a very neat script: *Meet me in Providence Park. I'll be waiting for you after 7 p.m. I may have important information. A. T.*

When it came to melodrama, the mysterious "A. T." was giving Dana a run for her money. Yet another witness to my poor nonna's presence at Miracolo on the morning of the murder? With expectations high and time short for the Festa della Repubblica, I tossed the note into a corner of the counter, turned back to my tomatoes, and promptly forgot about it.

By the time we opened, Choo Choo and Vera had taken down two tables and moved them to the storeroom, and crowded the others to make room for the tarantella. In their costumes, the waitstaff looked like a *National Geographic* piece on the Italians That Time Forgot. I was wearing a black jersey off-the-shoulder and above-the-knee dress with enough spandex in it to cling demurely. Tonight, my toque and jacket were white. The calamari were behaving themselves nicely, and at 6:30, Landon cued the tarantella music. Streamers fluttered, tambourines got rattled and whapped, and the customers clapped in time to the music. I snapped a bunch of pictures on my phone.

Drinks were served extravagantly, which probably accounted for the Festa being such a big hit. Landon had done two homemade pasta-making demonstrations with some surprisingly funny patter he'd worked out with Mrs. Crawford, who backed him up with the cheesiest Italian songs ever. The irony went over the customers' heads, apparently, and I could swear some were crying. "O Sole Mio" and the circulating scent of the *pomodoro* sauce were the closest we had ever come to pure Italian cliché.

Dana turned up in costume to show the right spirit, but when it came time for the next tarantella show, she didn't have a partner. Before I could say "That's Amore," Landon got me out of my chef jacket and toque, Jonathan was tying an apron around me, Paulette jammed a beribboned comb into my hair, and Vera handed me a tambourine.

So much for the slinky black dress.

Dana took one look at the troupe, and tried to get Landon to switch her to Jonathan as the most attractive male (she kept this reason to herself, but I knew it was what she was thinking). Landon said if *he* couldn't dance with him, neither could she (he kept this reason to himself but I knew it was what *he* was thinking). So Dana and I were stuck with each other, which was just the sort of thing good friends totally understand.

Then Landon cued the music, and I plunked my right fist on my hip and raised my tambourine arm, heading into the tarantella step. Habit made me want to get into character, so I tried imagining I had been bitten by a deadly tarantula and was dancing away the effects of the poison. Considering my life over the past few days, this was not so far-fetched, and I got into it.

As we launched into the tarantella do-si-do, we switched partners. Dana ended up with Choo Choo, who was very light on his feet, and I ended up with Alma, who was not. I started to study her footwork to understand what she didn't get about the rhythm. "Left foot, Alma, left foot," I whispered, and she performed some unintentionally impressive steps to catch up.

Someone should have told her to wear normal shoes tonight, not the latest pair of Art for Your Feet. But then I realized I'd seen this pair before. They were low heels with little red spangles, and enough silver studs and glitter to cause an overdose. But something was wrong. The last time she had worn them, you couldn't see the beige canvas beneath the "art."

Now one of the shoes looked like a dog with mange, with bald spots where the glue had failed. How had Alma missed that? I felt troubled, but couldn't figure out why.

At the end of the dance, customers started pushing the tables into one long table, like you find in VFW halls. As they launched into "When the moon hits your eye like a bigga pizza pie, that's *amore,*" I went back into my kitchen to check on the extra help we'd hired for the evening and give the *pomodoro* sauce and the *milanese* sauce a few good stirs.

Li Wei gazed longingly into the dining

room and I gave him a little nudge. "Go ahead, get in the next round of tarantella. Go on." There had to be some extra tambourines and sashes somewhere. Out he flew with a grateful look.

While I plated an order of the calamari special, Choo Choo stuck his flushed face through the doors. "You've been requested, *cara,*" he called. "Special." He explained that the addition of Li Wei threw the numbers off, but a guy at the bar said he could dance with me "just to even it up."

I set down my spoons with bad grace, blew the hair out of my face, and flipped the streamers back with my hand. So now I'm supposed to be the entertainment?

The crowd was now pounding their long table and yelling, "Eve! Eve!" to the sounds of Mrs. Crawford's lusty arpeggios.

I knew a cue when I heard one. I adjusted my off-the-shoulder dress, raked my hair, and stepped back out into the dining room, where our normally respectable patrons were standing on their chairs and knocking back grappas. A couple were harmonizing "Funiculì, funiculà, funiculì, funicu-LAH! Joy is everywhere —"

When the crowd saw me, you'd swear it was an appearance by Lady Gaga. People actually started flicking lighters. The wait staff dancers were now so full of themselves, you'd think no tarantula could fell them. Vera was twirling, Jonathan was doing some *Saturday Night Fever* moves, Landon was swooning, and Choo Choo was conducting the choir through their funiculis.

Then Landon cued the tarantella music and everybody partnered up, looking like Musical Chairs at a third-grade birthday party. I couldn't help laughing when Dana ended up with Li Wei, whose sash was wound mummylike around his skinny middle.

Which left me to look for the guy at the bar who apparently knew the tarantella and had asked for me, special. And then I saw him, dressed in a tailored black shirt and gray pants, coming toward me through the crowd, his hand extended.

It was Joe Beck.

18

When Joe's arm was around my waist I couldn't help remembering our not-so-fake kiss by the pod, which threw me off my tambourine rattles. So I thought about Arlen Mather, and from there I remembered my mysterious summons to a meeting in the park. When the song ended, a few customers decided they were ready to take on the tarantella and swarmed us. Within seconds, with claps and shouted instructions, Landon put a dance class together.

I returned to the kitchen, where I stood right on the spot where I had found Mather, casting my mind back to that morning. How I didn't recognize him; how I staggered around trying to make sense of a corpse on my kitchen floor. What else? I remembered accidentally turning on the Sinatra before Landon showed up. And for some reason I felt like I had cleaned up. But our cleaning service, Maid for You, had come during the night, and they're especially great with the floors.

I turned in a slow circle, trying to get the picture. It had something to do with a cake . . . yes! Landon had made a cassata cake the day before the murder, and some of his silver sugar pearls had gone unswept. Needing something to do with my trembling hands, I'd picked them up as I tried to process the fact that there was a corpse in my kitchen, and . . .

Ignoring the culinary frenzy around me, I went over to the junk corner of the counter. When I lifted up the new junk mail, there they were. But as I peered at the decorations, I realized with a sinking heart that they weren't silver sugar pearls. At all. They were little silver studs from what had to be Alma Toscano's shoes — and they were evidence in a crime . . .

I told myself not to jump to conclusions. Jumping was way too timid. I was catapulting to conclusions, which felt better in every way.

"Don't touch anything on this counter," I warned the kitchen staff, who nodded at me, distracted. Then I went straight to the office to check the shift list for the waitstaff. Maybe Alma had lost the silver studs while working the night before the murder, and

Maid for You just hadn't worked up to their usual standard. Yes, that was it. Most definitely.

My eyes scanned the shift list. On Monday, May 26, Alma Toscano had been the only server who *hadn't* worked. Before I dragged Joe into these mental gymnastics, I decided to get whatever information my mysterious pal had promised me. So I slipped on a light jacket, stuffed my phone in the front pocket, and headed toward the back door. "Don't touch anything on that junk counter," I yelled to the temporary help, and when they rolled their eyes I realized it was like telling the *Titanic* passengers to lay off the shuffleboard after the iceberg.

I walked briskly along the flagstone path at the side of the restaurant and discovered that the front door had been propped open and the sounds of our Festa party were spilling out to the street. It was probably just a matter of time before the cops showed up. In the light breeze, an Italian flag that could have been seen for miles from the top of a castle fluttered from a holder Choo Choo had mounted on the bricks.

As I crossed the street, a Channel 5 TV truck pulled up out front and double-parked. I hurried past, grateful Maria Pia

313

wasn't around to see her beloved restaurant become the Bad Boy of Market Square. The towering locust trees acted like a natural sound barrier, muffling the street noises from the peace of the park. I glanced at my watch. The note said anytime after 7 p.m., and it was nearly eight. I cut across the grass to the public path, then passed the playground, where a baby lay sleeping in a stroller next to a young woman reading a bodice ripper.

Could she be A. T.?

I lingered and finally gave it a shot. "Hi," I said meaningfully, "I'm Eve."

When all I got was a "Yah?" I decided she was not my note writer.

I passed an old man cleaning up after his dog, then a gaggle of twentysomethings commiserating over the sorry lot of local men. Not one of them eyed me, so I figured no A. T. On a bench at the far end of the park, hunched over her big, shapeless bag, was Akahana. I'd always smiled at her but never gotten much in return, so I was surprised when she suddenly looked up and declared, "Eve Angelotta."

I stopped in my tracks, then took a step closer. I felt like Moses at the moment he discovered plant life was capable of speech.

"I don't have all day," said Akahana. "Do

you want to talk or not?"

I drew closer. "Did you send me the note?"

"Of course I sent you the note," she barked. "I'm Akahana Takei — A. T." She fixed me with a stern look, then went on. "I saw someone enter your place the morning of the murder."

"You know about the murder?"

"I read the papers," she said. "Mostly the *New York Times,* but the locals for entertainment. I circle all the errors."

I frowned. "It's been almost a week. Why are you telling me now?"

If she were Italian, now was the moment she would have given me the two-handed gesture that says *The diameter of your head is two feet and it's filled with mascarpone.* "Because at first I thought it was your grandmother!" The "you ninny" was left unspoken. "But there were other witnesses, and I don't like to be troubled. Trouble interrupts my work. That morning, I made my way around Market Square and was in the alley by the Logan Building when I saw her again."

"And you thought it was my grand-mother."

She sat up as straight as she could. "I did. I really don't pay too much attention to

315

other people. They don't interest me, and I'm far too busy for that."

Busy Dumpster diving? "What do you do?" I asked, hoping I didn't sound too baffled.

"I'm writing a book on the origins of consciousness. I work at night."

I digested this bit of news. "So," I said, bringing the conversation back around to something I could actually talk about, "can you describe this woman who wasn't my grandmother?"

"Same height, same weight, same age."

Biting back a critique of Akahana's descriptive skills, I pulled out my phone and tapped to the pictures I had snapped during the tarantella. So as not to prejudice the witness, I showed her one of Vera. Akahana gave a tight shake of her head. "Not her." I showed her one of Paulette. She seemed to pause and consider. "Too short." I showed her one of Dana. "Not her."

When I showed her one of Alma Toscano, Akahana's face went flat and her hands went very still. After a few seconds, she said, "That one."

Alma. Maria Pia's old friend, Our Lady of Reduced Circumstances. But why?

I thanked Akahana and shook her hand. She promised me she'd talk to the cops, but only if they came to her, and she handed me a business card: Akahana Takei, PhD, Cognitive Anthropology. Three different phone numbers, two different email addresses, a website, and an address on West Fourth Street in Quaker Hills. I promised her a plate of my *fritto misto di pesce* the very next time I made it.

I found myself half running back to Miracolo. At the last Free Maria Pia meeting at Joe's place, Alma had jumped right in to research Max Scotti's past, maybe figuring she could fudge the info and lead us all away from the truth. But she hadn't called the dead guy "Max." She called him Maximiliano.

At the time I'd thought how funny it sounded, coming from the lips of flyaway old Alma, who probably never went anywhere more exotic than a local crap-for-crafts outlet. But it was easy not to see any further than the one, narrow little way I knew her. It was easy to overlook whatever else — about anyone — just didn't seem to apply.

What had happened to her husband? Did she have children? Where did she used to live before whatever disaster befell her, and she moved to low-income housing and took a waitressing job at her old friend Maria

317

Pia's place, where she could barely keep up? To me she was just Alma, with her minimalistic grooming and air of carrying a crushing burden that had nothing to do with platters of fine northern Italian food.

But somehow she had known the name Maximiliano. If she hadn't heard it that morning at Joe's, then that meant she knew the man. And if she knew the man, the question that was making me shudder was whether she had killed him.

But how was I going to figure that out?

Slipping around to the back of Miracolo, where groups of drunk, dancing customers and dancers were showing off for the local TV cameras, I tried to remember how we'd talked about Mather, which was the first time we learned his real name. Dana had reported to the group that she and Patrick had known him as a financial adviser, and that his name was Scotti. But did she say Max? Or Maximiliano?

Inside the double doors, I managed to get Joe's attention and pointed at Dana, who was clearly having a great old time in front of the camera. He whispered in her ear, and, amazingly, she tore herself away and headed right toward me. I could tell from her pumped-up expression that Festa della Repubblica would, in her mind, forever be known as her Triumphant Return. I had her complete attention for maybe the next five minutes.

I guided her into the back hall and gripped her upper arms. "Dana, that morning at Joe's. You know, the Free Maria Pia meeting?"

She nodded, radiating helpfulness.

"You reported on Max Scotti as a financial adviser you and Patrick had known, right?"

"Right." She blinked, distracted.

"Well, how did you refer to him?"

"What do you mean?" she asked with a frown.

I was dimming her Triumphant Return with these imponderables.

"Did you call him Maximiliano?"

She laughed, laying a hand on my arm. "Why would I call him that?"

Was I slow on the uptake? "Because it was his name?"

Dana smiled. "I called him Max. That's the only name I ever heard for him. It's how he introduced himself."

I stepped back. "Are you absolutely sure, Dana?"

She smoothed my hair. "Yes, darling, I'm sure. Now I've got to get back to my interview." And she was gone.

One last little thread . . .

I put a call through to Maid for You and got Marvin. Once I reassured him that I wasn't calling to cancel tonight's cleaning service, and that I had no complaints about any of the maids — not him, not Buddy, and not Derek — then he relaxed and listened to what I had to say. My question made him need to consult his booking ledger, and I heard him thumbing through the pages.

"Miracolo, Miracolo, Miracolo," he muttered, pronouncing it "Mira Cola." He finally found the booking for the Monday night before the murder. Marvin himself had been on the job. And no, nothing unusual to report. No silver bracelet in the dining room. No cake decorations or silver studs on the kitchen floor. He was absolutely sure, because he had taken the opportunity to try out his new shop vac and was pleased to report that it could suck up Yankee Stadium if he pointed it in the right direction. I thanked him and hung up.

So the kitchen floor was clean by the morning of the murder.

Which meant that Alma's shoes hadn't shed their studs until the time when she came in behind Arlen Mather, picked up our black marble mortar — my heart started pounding — and bashed in his head.

But was it enough for the police? There was Akahana's identification . . . there were the silver studs on the kitchen floor. I could dig for the link between Alma Toscano and Max Scotti, but wouldn't it still seem circumstantial? I needed more evidence, something so strong that it would trump whatever the cops had on Nonna.

It was time to call in some help.

Joe listened to me without saying a word while I laid it all out for him in Miracolo's office. The testimony of Akahana, Marvin, and Dana. The evidence of the silver studs at the crime scene. Then whatever we could dig up about Alma's connection to Max Scotti, except that might take some time — and Maria Pia was due to be arraigned in the morning. I started pacing, which didn't seem to help Joe's thinking.

The noise in the dining room suddenly started to become more distant, so we looked out the double-door windows into the nearly empty dining room. Going through to the front door, we watched Choo Choo and his flag disappear up the street in a crowd of customers fervidly singing the Italian national anthem with grappas in hand. Landon skipped along by Jonathan. Leo, the regular mandolin player, was at the front of the mob with a concertina. It was the barricade scene from *Les Mis,* but with a whole lot of alcohol and no particular ideals.

And then I heard the sirens.

Suddenly Joe turned to me. "What we need," he said urgently, "is a confession."

The perfect plan. We quickly plotted, and at the end of thirty seconds we each had our jobs in the sting operation. Joe went off to take care of his, which had something to do with Paulette and whoever turned up in the police cruiser.

I dashed back inside, past the few people still in the dining room. Mrs. Crawford, lost in a jazz riff. Paulette, standing in the open front doorway, watching the spectacle. Li Wei, in a tarantella trance despite the lack of music. A few elderly patrons tucking in to their tiramisu. And Alma Toscano, just sitting there.

Time to get ready. Operation Nab Alma was up and running.

I went into the kitchen and grabbed one of our glass dessert plates, then darted into the storeroom for a couple of clean white napkins, and the key item — the closest thing to thumbscrews for Alma that we could improvise. I ripped off my tarantella apron and hair comb and stashed them on a shelf.

I took two minutes to collect myself, doing some deep breathing and watching the second hand make its way around the face of my watch. When I was as collected as I was going to get, I slipped a jacket over my dress and, props in hand, went out to the courtyard to wait.

I only hoped Joe had done his job.

By prearrangement, I took a seat at the black wrought-iron table closest to the compost bin. The votive candle was burning low, but there were two tiki lights doing the job nearby. I set the glass plate, which I had covered with one napkin, in front of me, then set down the other napkin. Then Joe ran toward me along the side of Miracolo, pulled a chair closer to me and sat, setting down a bottle of beer and a couple of pistachio biscotti.

"Everything in place?" I asked him in a low voice.

"I think so."

Even though we were at the very back of the courtyard, I could still hear the commotion out on the street. Police flashers strobed through the side yard, and a bullhorn crackled.

The response was a swell of laughter.

I was strangely calm, my mind going back to the night when I had met Joe at this very spot, startling him as he balanced on the rim of the compost bin.

When I reminded him, and we were both picturing the moment he fell in, he winced.

"Ah, Kayla," I said heavily.

"It was nothing," he said, looking straight ahead.

I gave him a sidelong look. "Then it was nothing for three days."

"Three nights," he corrected.

"Ah — Kayla," I said.

"Why do you keep saying that?" Joe asked.

I shot him a pained look. "Because she just went by out front, waving Choo Choo's flag."

He grunted. "I get the impression she has a knack for maximum disturbance."

"Of me?"

"Of anything."

"Was she worth it?" I turned to look at him. "Worth jeopardizing whatever you've got going with the blond beauty?" I actually wanted to know. "I'm not asking judgmentally. Really, I'm not."

This last week had rocketed me right out of the judgmental zone. If Joe Beck wined, dined, and bedded the half of Quaker Hills that did not include me, why should I care?

"Blond beauty?" He looked like he was racking his memory.

"The good-looking blond you were here with the other night, with James and Olivia?"

Joe looked sincerely puzzled. "Are you talking about Anna Carson, my law partner?"

"You're running around with your *law* partner now?" It was out of my mouth before I knew it, with a little too much volume.

"What do you mean, running around?" He sounded indignant.

"Dating."

"Dating is not the same as running around," he said with lawyerly loftiness. "Eve, my marriage ended five years ago. I date. But my law partner and I have never dated, *and* we've never run around."

"Oh," I said softly. "I guess that settles it."

Just then the back door to Miracolo opened, and Alma Toscano stepped outside. Backlit, she somehow looked scary, and my pulse picked up. I couldn't tell whether it was from seeing Alma starting toward us, who suddenly seemd bigger than I had ever quite appreciated, or from the new direction in my conversation with Joe.

Alma reached the table, where she loomed

very large indeed. "Paulette said you wanted to see me?" She pushed at the Festa comb in her hair.

Now that she was here, she didn't look quite so scary. Which may well have made Arlen/Max let down his guard, and maybe I wasn't paying attention to the right things just then.

"Yes, Alma, have a seat," I said coolly. Joe indicated the chair across from us.

She sat, then asked in a panicked voice, "Am I losing my job?"

"Well . . ." I wasn't sure how to answer that.

Joe jumped in. "We have something serious to talk over," he said grimly, then accidentally knocked a biscotto off the table with his elbow. We both ducked to retrieve it.

"If your marriage ended five years ago," I hissed at him under the table, "why do you still wear a wedding ring?"

"I was taking it to an estate jeweler," he hissed back at me, snagging the fallen biscotto.

"Because of Kayla?" I whispered.

"Kayla was an aberration." Then he shot me a wicked smile. "Think of her as my FedEx guy."

I gasped. "You know about the FedEx guy?"

"Everyone knows about the FedEx guy."

We resurfaced at the same time. While I sat there trembling with embarrassment, Joe turned to Alma. "We want to talk to you about Arlen Mather. Eve?" he prompted.

I stared at him. This part of the sting was completely unrehearsed. Why wasn't *he* handling it? I didn't know what was admissible in a court of law. Well, there was only one way to say it.

"We know you killed Arlen Mather, Alma." With that, I sat back and tried to appear all-knowing. "And that his real name was Maximiliano Scotti."

She stammered, "I-I-don't know what you —"

"Dana called him Max at our last meeting. But you called him Maximiliano, something only his killer could know." I was on shaky ground with that, but it sounded good.

Joe kept up the pressure. "And you took on researching Scotti to control the information and lead us away from anything that would incriminate you."

"That's a lie!"

"Oh, really?" I overrode her. "It won't take the cops long to figure out how you knew him. And from there, it's a slam-dunk to know why you killed him." Although, speaking for myself, I didn't have a clue.

She just sat there, stony.

Then I drew back the napkin that covered the glass plate. In the low light, what looked like a scattering of little silver studs was exposed. And then I forgot my point.

Alma stared at the plate.

So did I.

Sensing an impasse, Joe pointed to the studs. "This is just half of what the cops recovered at the scene of the murder."

"So what?" she bluffed. "I didn't have anything to do with —"

And then Joe swept the beer bottle right off the table. In the mess of broken glass and spraying beer, he growled, "Quit stalling, Alma."

Dazzled by such fine misdirection, I dove under the table and wrestled Alma's right shoe off her foot. Scrambling to my feet, I held it up like a trophy and pointed triumphantly at the bald patch on the beige canvas vamp. "*This* is the shoe you were wearing the morning you killed him."

She made an unsuccessful swipe at it. "You have no right to —"

I backed out of reach. "You were so busy with the marble mortar, you never even noticed that your, er, craft glue failed you in your moment of homicidal need." Was I laying it on too thick?

Alma shot me a defiant glare. "You can't prove anything!" she jeered, jerking her head toward the silver studs on the plate. Her hand darted toward them.

When she made a grab for it, Joe quickly pulled it away and slipped the napkin back into place. "Oh, yes, we can. The report from the crime lab just came back, and those studs show glue, canvas residue, and scrapes from a small set of pliers. While you've been here tonight, the cops have been searching your apartment."

She looked trapped, and I almost felt sorry for her. Almost.

I leaned across the table. "Finding those pliers, and matching them to the studs found at the crime is just a matter of time. So why don't you tell us why you killed poor Arlen, my nonna's boyfriend, a fine man who made her happy?" How long would I have to trowel it on before she snapped? "He treated her like a queen and he loved Italian opera and Caruso, and Caruso records, and Caruso songs that were —"

She exploded. And not a moment too soon. I was about to nod off. "Oh, shut up!" she shouted. "Shut up, shut up, shut *up*!"

Shaking with fury, she pushed herself to her feet. "You stupid little self-important prig!" I tried to tell myself she must be referring to Joe, but she did happen to be glaring at me. "What do you know about any of it! What do you know about anything outside of your precious stupid kitchen and your impossible grandmother, who twirls around and rakes it in and — and — bestows pitiful jobs on needy friends who once had more money than any of you will *ever* have!"

Joe and I sat very still while she hit her stride, describing how she and Jack Toscano, the sweetest, gentlest man on the face of this earth had been a high-powered Philadelphia society couple until that thief Maximiliano Scotti came along as their financial adviser. He had lost and mismanaged what he couldn't just plain steal of their money, sailing close enough to the wind to avoid prosecution and finally disappearing. But not before Jack, after a few years of not being able to climb out of the ruins of their life, killed himself. In front of her. *That's* what she'd had to live with. Every single day.

"When Scotti turned up again, calling himself Arlen Mather, he didn't recognize me. Why would he?" Alma's shaking hands swept through the air around her. "Look what he had made me!" She choked back a sob. "I even waited on him once, one night when you were off," she jerked her chin at me, "and he still didn't recognize me. So then I bided my time, following him — until last week." She had a satisfied, faraway look in her eye.

Alma stood very tall, and I saw a flash of her former self. "After Maria Pia dropped him off out front, I quietly followed him inside, into the kitchen, and picked up the mortar. When he finally heard me and started to turn, I told him this was for Jack. And then I brought it down on his head. Again and again and again." She let out a sigh of pleasure. "I haven't felt that good since Jack and I attended the ribbon cutting for the Toscano Psychiatry wing at St. Joseph's Hospital." She gazed at us serenely.

I heard a sound behind me, and a uniformed cop came out from behind the compost bin. As he handcuffed Alma and read her her rights, Joe and I grinned at each other in relief. The Festa della Repubblica revelers spilled into the courtyard, but when they saw what was going down, even the concertina stopped. As Alma limped away in the cop's firm grip, she suddenly reached down, whipped off her remaining shoe, and hurtled it away from her. And then I saw Choo Choo take off through the crowd, and I smiled. He'd arrive at the police station well before the cruiser pulled up with Alma Toscano inside.

19

I sat alone at the table in the back of the courtyard, listening to the night sounds. Everyone had departed. Joe had taken off after Choo Choo, and Landon had taken off after Joe. Some of the revelers replaced the flag, while others called cabs. A few went back into the dining room and settled up their bills. And Paulette and Giancarlo brought me a shot of Laphroaig on a silver tray. Apparently they had fought over who got to present it.

Our beloved regulars drifted in at the usual time. The night air was warm, and I closed my eyes. I could hear the deep thrum of the bass, and a run on the bongos. Even the clarinet had shown up. Dana was warming up with scales, and I thought how wonderful it was to love something so much that it really didn't matter if you weren't very good at it. Mrs. Crawford was still at the piano, and it finally felt like this was the known world, after all.

Miracolo and Market Square and my beloved family.

Though I no longer needed legal services from my lawyer, that didn't rule out other possibilities. I imagined us dancing alone in the courtyard, I in my hot red sheath, he in his floral swim trunks, while Mrs. Crawford turned "Your Eyes Have Told Me What I Did Not Know" into dance music.

As I finished my shot, I heard a distant commotion and what sounded like a drum-roll made by dozens of hands. Shouts of joy went up inside. I stood up with a smile and headed back to the inviting lights of our restaurant. In the dining room, I heard a familiar voice complaining about that *strega* Alma Toscano, killer of perfectly nice boyfriends.

I'd die before I'd ever tell her that the perfectly nice boyfriend had called her an "elderly friend" to Calladine.

Then the raggedy little band started up, and as I stood for one minute longer inside the doors to the dining room, Landon popped his head in to say that Joe had gone home. That was okay; I could thank him later. The musicians started playing "Three Coins in the Fountain," and our two divas started bellowing out the words.

When I pushed open the double doors, there she was, her fresh lipstick a little smudged, her skirts fully deployed as she twirled around the floor. My nonna. Sprung.

I headed over toward her . . . but there was the little matter of the cannoli, and I hesitated.

She caught sight of me then, stopped twirling, and stopped trying to outdo Dana. And without any hesitation, my nonna came over to me, spread her arms wide, and took me in.

EVE'S RECIPE FOR
THE REBEL CANNOLI

You can purchase cannoli tubes online or at a specialty store. They come in packages of four, and each tube measures 1×8″.

For the Shell:

1 1/2 cups all-purpose flour

2 tablespoons granulated sugar

1 1/2 tablespoons butter, cut into pieces

1 egg, separated

1/4 cup Soave or Pinot Grigio (both are from northern Italy, so Maria Pia would at least approve of the wine, if not the cannoli)

1 1/2 teaspoons white vinegar

1 tablespoon water

Mix the flour and sugar. Cut in the butter. Into an indentation in the center, add the egg yolk, just *half* the egg white (set aside the remainder), the wine, vinegar, and water. Mix to form a dough, then knead for

10 minutes. Cover and chill for an hour. On a floured surface, roll out the dough nearly paper thin. Then cut the dough into rounds (about 3–4 inches' diameter) using the rim of a margarita glass.

Roll each round securely around a cannoli tube. Beat a little water into the remaining egg white. Where the dough overlaps, brush both the underside and the topside with the slightly beaten egg white to seal. Fry in deep, hot canola oil (about 350°) until golden. Watch carefully! Remove and drain on paper towels. When cool enough to handle, slide each cannoli shell off its tube. Let cool completely before filling.

For the Filling:
2 cups whole milk ricotta cheese
1/3 cup powdered sugar
1/2 teaspoon vanilla extract
1/8 cup dark chocolate, shaved
1 ounce chocolate liqueur
1/2 cup heavy cream

Drain the ricotta well. Combine the ricotta, powdered sugar, and vanilla extract. Add the shaved chocolate and chocolate liqueur. Whip the heavy cream to stiff peaks, then fold into the mixture. Chill the filling for about 30 minutes before piping into cooled cannoli shells. Sprinkle additional chocolate or powdered sugar on top, if you like.

Tips:

1. Eve loves the double chocolate effect of the shaved dark chocolate ("Is there any other kind?") and chocolate liqueur in this recipe, but you can substitute Frangelico, a hazelnut liqueur from northern Italy, if you want to go nuts.
2. Don't preassemble your cannoli because the shells will get soggy. Instead, fill the shells close to the serving time, and refrigerate.
3. Use a regular pot for deep frying the shells. Deep fryers (without settings) get too hot and pop the shells apart.
4. If you don't have a pastry bag, you can use a Ziploc® bag by snipping off a corner!